JUST A
MOMENT

CHANGES LIFE FOREVER

ENDORSEMENTS

As you turn the pages of this beautifully written historical novel, prepare to fall in love with people you will never meet but soon will feel like family. Reading *Just a Moment*, I felt as if I had entered a time machine, living in an America of purity, morality, hardship, and resolve, now sadly long forgotten. All these beautiful attributes of a now divided America might have perished had it not been for the Antiques Roadshow style "barn discovery" of a diary and letters about the Catts/Crawford family. It made me want to bury my computer and lick a stamp on a letter to those I love. Billie Fulton will long be remembered for this great timeless literary work.

—**Ron Hall**, #1 *New York Times* bestselling author, screen writer/producer of the book and movie *Same Kind Different As Me*. Also host of the Ron Hall Show (ronhallshow.com).

"I am a fan of anything that Billie Fulton writes!"
—**Jennifer Rothschild**, Author of *Me, Myself and Lies*

If you enjoy genealogy, history, family stories, and faith, you're going to love *Just a Moment* by Billie Fulton. Settle down on the porch swing with a glass of iced tea and your copy and join the Catts and Crawfords as they follow their dreams and become new settlers. Celebrate their joys, mourn their sorrows, and be inspired by God's faithfulness throughout their lives. You'll be glad you came along for the journey.

—**Michelle Cox**, bestselling author of *Just 18 Summers* and the *When God Calls the Heart* series

Billie Fulton writes enjoyable fiction about young people discovering their family history. In *Just a Moment*, three grandchildren visit Pops and Grams at their farm and Lydia stays for a longer visit ... "A place where they could find hidden treasures from the past, enjoy the present, and question the future." An old and mysterious box attracts the attention of Lydia, who simply must find the key to its contents. Grams encourages Lydia's search, and they find common ground in their shared struggles with dyslexia. Eventually, Lydia finds an antiquarian diary which sets the plot in motion, as snippets from the diary move the story along throughout the book. This became a fast read for me, which indicates it would work well for adults who enjoy clean, Christian fiction and for younger teens. I appreciate Fulton's writing and the innocence of her stories. Like Horton Foote, she takes her time telling a story and allows the reader to come along for a journey of discovery. Highly recommend *Just a Moment*.

—**David L. Winters**, author and speaker, *A Baby's Right to Choose: A Novel*

Mrs. Fulton's book is a treasure. It is a great family history story!! The places, historical figures, and dates are accurate, and the description of the local Ozark area is spot on. I wish I had as much information on my own family history as Fulton has on the Catts/Crawford family. A great read for anyone interested in Ozark/family history!

—**Connie Langum**, Wilson's Creek National Battlefield Historian

Have you ever wondered where we, our nation, our culture are going? If you sometimes think we are lost or heading in the wrong direction, it is well to look back over our shoulder and see from whence we came. In *Just a Moment,* Billie Fulton takes us along on a journey with the Catts/Crawford family from the cradle of our infant nation to its western frontier. It is a journey of faith when faith was often all the family had to sustain them. Their faith will nurture you as well.

—**Sam Jones**, Lawrence County Missouri Judge

Billie Fulton takes the readers on an inspiring story full of history and determination. I highly recommend taking the journey with Lydia and Jane Ann to watch them grow confidently despite their dyslexia struggles. As the story unfolds, Lydia learns about Gram's and Jane Ann's reading struggles and that she is not alone. She too finds out through determination and hard work, she can become a better reader. Dyslexia affects everyone differently, but the appreciation that it is being discussed more will be helpful to many new learners.

—**Marla McKan**, M. Ed., CALT-QI, Springfield Center for Dyslexia & Learning

Just a Moment—a deliciously heartwarming story of present-day Lydia, a young dyslexia girl, and Jane Ann Catts, born in the early 1800s. Through the diary entries of Jane Ann, Lydia comes to realize Jane must have struggled with dyslexia. Lydia is inspired, that with Jesus's help, she too can overcome her own disability. The reader will find hope in this feel good story that connects us to the past."

—**Penelope Childers**, co-author of *A Cry of the Heart: Human Trafficking, One Survivor's True Story*

Billie drew me into her pages and touched my spirit. I grieved with her characters, laughed with them, cheered them on, and learned from them. A wonderful read.

—**Ruth Marshall**, wife of Dr. John Marshall

I love this book! It is so entertaining. The characters are so well developed. It is extremely easy to get intertwined and wrapped up with this family. Grab a hot cup of good coffee and you will soon realize it is hard to put *Just A Moment*, down. You want to know everything about each character and how they fit into the timeline of American history. Might there be another book?

—**Jacque Summers**, co-owner of Churchill's Coffee Company

A tale which creatively depicts the lives of a pioneer family who confront adventure, hardship, and change with enduring love, unwavering faith, and

eternal hope. The author's ability to weave plausible emotion with historical facts makes the characters and setting come alive for the contemporary reader.
—**Mary Etta**, friend and encourager.

JUST A
MOMENT

CHANGES LIFE FOREVER

Billie Fulton
ILLUSTRATED BY JOHN FULTON

ELK LAKE PUBLISHING INC

PUBLISHING THE POSITIVE
Plymouth, Massachusetts

Cover and Interior Design: Derinda Babcock

Editor(s):Jeanne Marie Leach, Deb Haggerty

Interior Illustrations: John Fulton

PUBLISHED BY: Elk Lake Publishing, Inc., 35 Dogwood Drive, Plymouth, MA 02360, 2020

Library Cataloging Data
Names: Fulton, Billie (Billie Fulton)
Just a Moment—Changes Life Forever / Billie Fulton
254 p. 23cm × 15cm (9in × 6 in.)
Identifiers: ISBN-13: 978-1-64949-093-3 (paperback) |
978-1-64949-094-0 (trade paperback)
| 978-1-64949-095-7 (e-book)
Key Words: History, Civil War, Family, Faith, Journaling, Missouri, Dyslexia
LCCN: 2020952201 Fiction

DEDICATION

To God, I am forever grateful.

To our granddaughter, Lydia, and to every person with dyslexia who sees their challenges as a gift.

To my forever hero, my husband John.

To my friend and encourager, Mary Etta Giles.

To Jane Ann Catts/Crawford and Robert W. Crawford who left their inspiring story for me to find.

Col. *Robert(White) Crawford* Wife of *Robert W. Crawford* *Jane Ann (Catts) Crawford*

Photos provided by
C. M. Crawford
Calvary Commander United States Army, Retired
Great-great-grandson of
Colonel Robert W. Crawford

ACKNOWLEDGMENTS

I want to thank Lydia, who teaches me every day that no challenge is bigger than the God we serve.

To my husband John, who encouraged me to step out in faith to see all God can accomplish with a willing heart. I love you forever.

To Tate, Pru, Silas, and Pricilla Rose whose inspiration I have hidden within this story. And to their parents, Kelli, Jason, Cassi, and Chad who prayed me through to the last page.

To Deb Haggerty, Publisher and Editor-in-Chief at Elk Lake Publishing, Inc. Your God given wisdom and guidance kept me encouraged to the last celebrated words of this book, "The End." I am forever grateful for the opportunity to publish with you.

To Derinda Babcock, Graphic Designer, Elk Lake Publishing. Your creativity on the cover and layout is perfect. Thank you.

To Jeanne Marie Leach, Editor and Writing Coach, Elk Lake Publishing. Your talent and guidance challenged me to search my heart deeper in my writing. Thank you.

To the Catts/Crawford family who stepped out to be counted as American Patriots and pioneers. Your strong spirit of courage and foundation of faith remains on the farm your family homesteaded in 1839.

To Juanita and L. D. Fulton who prayer walked the farm and dedicated the land to God again in 1945. Their example is lovingly woven throughout the pages of each chapter. I am forever thankful for their love.

To my sisters, Freda, Carole, and Edie, who always believed in me. And in loving memory of my beloved brother, Bill. I love you all.

Finally, to the many, many friends who are my treasures in life. Thank you all.

For where your treasure is, Billie, there your heart will be also. Matthew 6:21

PROLOGUE

Life can be changed in just one simple moment. A birth, a marriage, a death, or an encouraging word can change a life forever. Lydia, a young ten-year-old girl challenged with dyslexia has a life changing moment when she finds a hidden key in the Catts/Crawford family Bible. The key takes her on a journey back in time through the pages of a young girl's diary. Here she discovers they are much the same, only two-hundred years apart in the time they lived.

Lydia walks with her newly found friend as she travels more than one-thousand miles to Missouri. Step by step, she experiences with her friend the history of America, Missouri, and the farm her grandparents now own. And in just a moment her life was forever changed when she understands her dyslexia as a gift instead of a challenge.

CHAPTER 1

The peaceful silence of a cool summer evening was interrupted only by the squeaking sound of a worn chain on the porch swing. Slowly swinging back and forth, Pops and Grams Fulton waited. Wooster, Pop's farm dog, lay sleeping beside his feet. Suddenly, Wooster's tail started to wag, and his head popped up. They saw car lights coming up the quarter-mile gravel lane leading to the old Fulton farmhouse.

Grams and Pops jumped to their feet as the car turned into the driveway. The grandkids, Lydia, Silas, and Priscilla Rose had arrived.

As with every visit to the Fulton farm, a new adventure awaited the children. For a child, the farm was a vast frontier where they could explore and let their imaginations run free. A place where they could find hidden treasures from the past, enjoy the present, and question the future. A place of refuge to experience the wonder of a simple life. Sometimes they found tangible treasures to take home. But most often they discovered life lessons which became enduring treasures.

After a night of rest and Grams's breakfast on the porch, Pops lead the kids on their adventure.

While exploring the woods, Silas found the hub of a wooden wagon wheel covered in ivy leaning against a tree. He imagined it belonged to a pioneer who once traveled west.

Priscilla Rose soon went back to the house to stay with Grams. They pilfered through her drawers of keepsakes searching for a treasure she wanted to take home. She found a set of embroidered rose pillowslips Grams made when she was a little girl.

Grams told Priscilla Rose, "I would be delighted if you would like to take them home."

With a shy sweet smile, she responded, "Yes, please."

Knowing her parents had been searching for a new bedroom set for Lydia, Pops asked Lydia, "Would you walk with me to the barn? I'd like to show you something you might want." As they walked into the barn, Pops continued, "For as long as I can remember, over here in the corner has been an antique bedroom set that was left in the barn when my parents bought the farm in 1945."

The furniture was covered in tarps and wrapped in oil cloth for protection.

Lydia's dad helped Pops unwrap the furniture to see if it was something Lydia would like to have for her bedroom. Under the dusty, faded tarp they discovered a bed frame, a chest, and a vanity dresser with a mirror and a bench made of walnut wood.

As soon as Lydia looked at the vanity and bench, she knew she wanted the set for her room.

"It's yours, Lydia. But it will most likely need to be sanded, repaired, and oiled." Pops said.

This visit to the farm would be different for Lydia than the others. She would not go home with her family but instead be allowed to stay with Grams and Pops for two weeks. She had been waiting for a tough school year to end, so she was more than excited to stay with her grandparents. She hoped what bothered her would be left behind if only for two weeks.

After hearing the weather report, they realized rain was going to occur most of the week. Lydia's Dad and Pops decided to carry the furniture to the big, covered, front porch. They put the set on tarps and treated around the furniture with an organic bug spray as a safety precaution. The spacious porch would be a perfect place to work when it rained.

The next day was a bittersweet time for Lydia, saying goodbye to her family. She tried to keep her smile as she stood between Grams and Pops, waving until they turned on the highway.

Noticing Lydia was fighting back tears, Grams ad Pops looped their arms around her and swung her up onto the steps of the porch. She was laughing as they went inside.

"Lydia, I'm making your favorite cornbread pie for dessert."

Excitedly, she asked Grams, "Will you teach me to cook while I'm at the farm?"

"I certainly will," Grams responded, pleased she would ask.

After supper, as was the evening ritual, they moved out onto the porch to watch the pond in front of the house. They waited to see which animals meandered out of the woods to be their evening entertainment. "I wonder what we will see tonight," Pops said.

Lydia was quiet and looked a little like she might be missing her family, so Pops started making croaking sounds like the frogs sitting around the pond. In harmony, he bounced the sound back and forth with the frogs while the crickets chirped along.

Lydia laughed in delight. Tired after the long trip from Tennessee and a full weekend with family at the farm, she yawned and stretched her arms.

"I'd say it's time for bed." Grams said.

Before she went inside, Lydia glanced at the furniture sitting on the tarp. "Pops, could we work on the furniture in the morning?"

He nodded. "But first, I have to get the hay baled before the rain comes."

"Good night, Pops." Lydia smiled, gave him a hug, and headed to bed.

Grams followed her inside to tuck her in.

With the cool fresh air flowing from the open window, Lydia snuggled under a soft quilt and fell asleep praying for her family.

The next morning Lydia awoke to Grams singing from the hallway. "Good morning, Lydia sunshine, how did you wake so soon? You scared all the birds awake and shined away the moon."

Lydia laughed. This was how she'd been told Grams woke up Lydia's mom when she was a little girl.

By this time, Pops had already eaten breakfast. Lydia went into the kitchen as Pops stood and announced, "I have to make hay while there's still sunshine." Picking up a jug of water, he hurried out the back door to the barn.

Lydia watched from the kitchen window as he pulled his tractor and bailer out of the barn and headed to the field. Since she was little, she'd loved the roaring sound of Pops' tractor and seeing the huge hay bales left behind by the bailer.

"Let's make vanilla oatcakes for breakfast," Grams said. "You can help."

"Oh, good!" Lydia topped them with a sprinkle of brown sugar, cream, and chopped pecans.

After cleaning the kitchen, they grabbed a bucket and walked out to the garden to pick tomatoes and other vegetables. They enjoyed small talk and laughing until Grams asked, "Lydia, how did school go this year?"

Lydia wasn't ready to answer that question and didn't know what to say. They were silent for a few agonizing, uncomfortable moments.

"Wooster!" Grams suddenly called. Looking at Lydia, she asked, "Want to see how high Wooster can jump?" Grams tossed a ripe tomato high above Wooster as he came running through the grass. He jumped and caught the tomato in his front teeth. Juice and seeds sprayed from his mouth.

Lydia laughed and tossed another tomato Wooster's way.

Hearing the barn door close, she saw Pops walking toward the garden.

He called out to them, "I'm hungry and ready for lunch. I've had a long morning in the hay field."

They went inside for lunch. Soon rain gently tapped against the kitchen windows.

After he finished eating, Pops headed for his comfortable chair, but Lydia had other plans. She grabbed his hand. "Can we work on my furniture now?" Without any resistance from Pops, she led him out onto the porch.

"Let's line up the furniture on the tarp so we can take a better look at what we are getting ourselves into," Pops said. He walked around, giving a knock here and a tap there to see how sturdy each piece was. He pulled out each drawer to check if the glides worked.

Grams came out of the house with a box of rags and said with a smile, "We can use these for cleaning the furniture inside and out. I like everything clean and neat."

Lydia had already started to pull away the oil cloth covering the bench. "Oh, wow! This'll look nice in my room." The cushion on the bench had a needlepoint covering of variegated roses.

"That would explain why the bench was covered so well," Grams said as she rubbed her hand across the cushion. "Needlework like this takes a lot of skill and a long time to complete."

"You mean someone actually stitched this by hand?" Lydia asked.

6

"Yes," Grams answered, "Mothers use to teach their young daughters how to do needlework so they could make their clothes and sew for their families. This is exceptional work."

The three of them stepped back to evaluate where to start.

"I think keeping the natural walnut color would be best, don't you?" Pops asked.

Lydia and Grams both agreed, so they started right to work.

Pops gathered sandpaper and the tools they'd need to complete their job, and then set them out of the way. "First, we need to disassemble everything," he said. "Let's start by removing the drawers, handles, and knobs."

Next, Pops removed the mirror from the vanity while Lydia sat on the bench to see how comfortable it might be. With admiration, she carefully let her fingers glide across the needlepoint seat cover.

"Hmm," Grams said. "There's an old paper label glued on the back of the mirror that reads, "Springfield Furniture Company, 601 North National, Springfield, Missouri." She gathered loose papers and fabric from inside the drawers.

The porch was a perfect place to stay dry while they worked on the furniture. A cool breeze refreshed them while they listened to the raindrops hitting the metal roof of the barn.

Pops turned his attention to the bed while Grams sanded the chest.

Lydia worked on the vanity, and as she sanded the last drawer, she suddenly felt something move on the back side. Thinking it might be a bug or a spider, she squealed at the same time a clap of thunder sounded in the distance, scaring her even more.

Startled, Grams asked, "Are you okay?"

"I don't know. I felt something move." Lydia said as she turned the drawer on end.

She found a skeleton key swinging back and forth on a screw. Pops unscrewed the screw, and the key fell into Lydia's hand.

"I wonder what it goes to?"

Pops examined the front of each drawer. "I don't see any keyholes. Perhaps the key opens a treasure," he said with a grin.

Lydia tucked the key into her pocket. She thought about the mysteries her cousin, Tate, had unlocked with the keys he found there last year.

Grams and Pops started to rub the furniture with mineral oil. With every swipe of the cloth, the curling and burling of the walnut looked more beautiful.

Pops suggested Lydia might want to sand the bench so it would be ready to oil. He picked up a screwdriver to remove the cushion so oil wouldn't damage the needlepoint.

Lydia sat on the tarp on the floor and gently rubbed sandpaper along the edges of the bench. She felt an odd bump on the wood. Leaning closer, she turned her head sideways and saw a keyhole. "Why would there be a keyhole on the edge of a bench?" she asked out loud.

Glancing at Grams, Lydia could tell she too was surprised. Pops bent over to look at what she found.

"Maybe," Pops mumbled, "just maybe, this is what the key you found will unlock."

Lydia pulled the key out and inserted it into the keyhole under the edge of the cushion. The lock clicked.

Pushing up on the cushion, Pops discovered it was hinged like a piano bench. Inside were stacks of papers, some loose items, a tapestry drawstring bag, and a rectangular wooden box. Looking at Grams for approval, Lydia picked up the box.

"That box looks to be very old and made from cherry wood." Pops commented.  "Why don't you check the bottom? They used to carve the date and sometimes their initials on the bottom."

As Lydia turned the box over, she could hear things moving inside. On the bottom was carved, "J. N. 1814." She handed the box to Pops, and he showed her there was a lock on the front.

They all three stood silent, pondering who J. N. might be and where they might find the key.

Pops interrupted their deep thoughts saying, "It's been a long day, and I'm going in to catch the news before supper."

Grams found a wash basket in which to put the items from the bench, and Lydia carried the basket inside.

Lydia and Grams prepared a summer supper of fresh garden vegetables and ice-cold watermelon. "Pops, come eat," they called. After the prayer, Lydia couldn't stop talking about the hidden key and the hiding place under the bench cushion.

With supper finished, the kitchen cleaned, and Pops in his recliner asleep, Grams and Lydia quietly carried the wash basket to her bedroom. Grams laid a tattered old quilt over the bed so they could sort the items without getting the bedspread dirty.

They stacked the papers together and placed the loose items into a pile but found no key. As she handed the stack of papers to Lydia, Grams suggested, "Why don't we sort these by dates?"

Lydia tried but quickly became frustrated and covered her eyes.

Grams pulled her close. "Can't you see the letters and numbers?"

Lydia kept her eyes covered and replied, "I can see them, but I can't tell what they are. They are all jumbled. That's why the kids at school tease me."

Grams slid off the bed to her knees and pulled Lydia's hands from her eyes. Wrapping her arms around Lydia, she whispered, "I have dyslexia too."

Shocked and confused, Lydia said, "But you don't seem to have any of the problems I have."

Grams smiled. "When I was learning to read, the letters would mix up and go backward. I could see the letters, but my brain couldn't understand them."

"That's exactly what happens to me all the time," Lydia admitted to Grams. "When I have to read out loud, I get upset when I stumble on the words. One boy teases me when our teachers aren't in the room."

Grams hugged Lydia close and compassionately said, "Oh, sweet Lydia, I know your parents help you and have a tutor working with you. Like me, your eyes and brain will meet one day. You'll still have challenges, but you can learn to work around them."

"Some of the most brilliant people throughout history have been dyslexic," Grams continued. She reached over to turn the side lamp on. "Thomas Edison, who invented the light bulb, was dyslexic. He also invented the first motion picture camera, which dyslexic Walt Disney used to make the movies you love to watch. Your dad likes to watch the Star Wars movies directed by Stephen Spielberg, and Tim Tebow is Pops's favorite football player. Lydia, they are both dyslexic. Alexander Graham Bell invented the first telephone, and Steve Jobs invented our Apple iPhone and computer. They were also dyslexic.

"You love to paint and create things. The Italian painter Leonardo da Vinci, who painted the famous Mona Lisa and the Last Supper of Jesus, was dyslexic. They saw and understood things others could never see."

Grams took Lydia's hands in hers and said, "I think you and I are in the company of some of the most brilliant people ever born."

Lydia smiled. "I didn't know you were dyslexic or that so many famous people were."

Looking into Lydia's eyes, Grams declared, "Only God knows all the amazing things he has for your future. As did they, you'll see things and create things others could never imagine.

"When I was your age, I memorized the Scripture, Jeremiah 29:11. I would fill in my name to claim the verse as God's promise to me. Listen, and I will fill in your name as your promise from God.

"'For I know the plans I have for you, Lydia, declares the Lord, plans to prosper you and not to harm you, plans to give you hope and a future.'"

Suddenly Wooster started barking.

"I wonder what's causing him to be upset," Grams said, as she and Lydia hurried to the living room to investigate.

As they walked into the room, Pops woke from a sound sleep and jumped to his feet. He flipped on the porch lights and peeked out the window. "I don't see anything," he said. Then he turned off the porch and inside lights. Shining a bright flashlight through the window around the porch, they could see two beady little eyes staring at them.

"Ah," Pops said, "a curious raccoon."

The animal immediately scurried away into the darkness.

Stretching, Pops said, "I forgot to cover the furniture."

He grabbed a new tarp and went out to take care of the task. Grams and Lydia followed.

The rain had stopped for a while. However, in case it started again during the night, they brought the bench inside. Propping the cushion up, Lydia felt around inside to be sure they'd found everything. As she rubbed her hand across the inside, she yelped.

"Ouch! Something scraped my finger."

Grams looked at her finger while Pops felt inside the bench. "Hmm. I think I know what scratched your finger." He looked at Grams, raised his eyebrows, and handed Lydia a flashlight. "Look inside at the left corner."

Shining the light as she carefully touched the spot where she'd scraped her finger, she declared, "There's a little nail with something hanging on it." Lydia wiggled the nail back and forth. Freeing it from its hiding place, she held up a key for Grams and Pops to see.

"What do you suppose this is for?" she asked. "Wait! I have an idea." Lydia ran to the bedroom for the wooden box she'd found inside the bench. Setting it down on a side table, she put the key into the lock and moved it back and forth until she heard a clicking sound. She pushed at the top. The lid opened.

Excited about what was inside, they all three leaned over the box, bumping their heads together. While they laughed at themselves, Lydia lifted up a brown-leather book from the box. Holding it under a light, she could see a lock on the side. Near the top was the word, "Diary," and across the bottom were gold embossed letters. Rubbing each letter, Lydia softly read each one.

"J-a-n-e A-n-n."

Pops spoke up, "I think that's one of the names from the Catts/Crawford cemetery in the hay field."

"It must be the diary of Jane Ann Catts/Crawford." he exclaimed. "Tate found her mother, Frances Catts-Crawford's, journal upstairs in an antique chest. The diary explained her life and pioneer journey to Missouri."

Lydia could hardly contain her excitement. "Ooh, I hope this diary has important information in it like the one Tate found."

Grams looked at Pops and declared, "Here we go again." She stepped into the dining room, moved the bouquet of flowers Lydia had picked from the garden that morning, and folded her mother's lace tablecloth.

"What are you doing, Grams?" Lydia asked.

"I'm laying out the same old tablecloth we used for Tate so we won't soil my good one. Now, let's organize the items and start looking for another key."

Lydia picked up the diary and placed it in the center of the table. She carefully placed the other items from the box beside the diary.

Grams returned with the items that were in the bench while Pops found some paper and a pen.

"What's that for, Pops?" Lydia asked.

"We need to keep a list of everything we find. It'll help us put the pieces of our new puzzle together."

"First," Pops said, "let's list the pieces of furniture found in the barn." He googled the Springfield Furniture Company and found it was in business from 1895 to 1933. "So, we know the furniture is somewhere between eighty-seven to one hundred twenty-five years old."

Grams pulled out an old Bible and showed it to Lydia. "This is the one Tate found in a wooden box from the attic." She turned to the Catts/Crawford family history in the center of the Bible.

"This is interesting. I never noticed this before.

Beside Jane Ann's name is written, *The key is in God's Word*. Now what do you think that could mean?" Grams asked. She looked over at Pops and then at Lydia and laid the Bible on the table.

To sort the items found in the bench, Grams placed a container on the left of the diary for them and one on the right for what was in the wooden box.

Lydia called out each item for Pops to note before carefully placing them in the container.

A small song book, a tapestry drawstring bag, which contained a gold bracelet, wrapped in a linen handkerchief with "Mother" embroidered on the corner. Also, a large skeleton key with a note attached. Lydia read out loud, "This key belongs to someone's future." She shrugged and laid it in the container.

Lydia next lifted out four letters and a bundle of papers with "Robert W. Crawford, Attorney at Law" on the front.

She pulled out what Pops thought looked like a floorplan drawing of the farmhouse dated 1885. Scribbled on the bottom was the name, Fannie Catts.

Sandwiched between two pieces of brown paper, Lydia found a pencil drawing of a woman. A note on the back said, "Fannie Catts, 1858, Wellsburg Women's Academy."

Pops separated out the floor plan. "I want to look at this later." He surmised, "Maybe there's a story about Fannie Catts from the items in the bench and another about Jane Ann from the items in the box and her diary."

While reaching for the wooden box, Lydia reminded Pops, "Don't forget to add the diary to your list." She called out each item one by one.

In the wooden box where the diary was found, Lydia counted seven letters. In the black velvet bag, she found a silver writing pen, a silver pocket watch, a silver baby spoon with the initials 'C. C.', a silver compass, and a silver sewing thimble. In the bottom of the bag was a beautiful blue broach wrapped in a handkerchief with the initials F.S.K. And strangely, in the bottom of the wooden box was a handful of thick red and white threads.

Pops laid his pad and pen on the table and patted Lydia on the back. "You girls have found some valuable treasures that have sat in the barn for many years. I'm tired and going to bed." Pops yawned then kissed Grams on her cheek and Lydia on the head and said, "Goodnight, girls."

"Goodnight," they said in unison while continuing to look at what they found for a minute or two more.

Grams leaned over and hugged Lydia tightly. She whispered, "Goodnight, God bless you. Remember, I love you." Off they went to bed.

Looking out the open window at the soft moonlight, Lydia thought about what Grams had shared. Was it possible for her to learn how to cope with her dyslexia? She'd never thought so before, but now a little hope sparkled in her heart.

MS. JUANITA'S VANILLA OAT CAKES

2 Cups of cooked thick cut oats
1 Cup of flour
1 Cup brown sugar
1 Tbs Vanilla
1 egg
¼ Cup oil
½ Cup milk
Mix all ingredients together. Cover bottom of large skillet with olive and heat. Spoon the mixture in circles like pancakes. Cook on both sides until golden brown.

Serve with a sprinkle of brown sugar, chopped pecans and a little milk.

CHAPTER 2

Lydia jumped out of bed to the sound she hoped to hear—rain dripping in the barrel at the corner of the porch. That sound would keep Pops inside for the day. She quickly dressed, combed her hair, and followed the aroma of cinnamon to the kitchen.

In the middle of the table sat a platter of homemade raised cinnamon rolls, topped with pecans and fresh raspberries.

"Mm. This looks and smells wonderful, Grams," she said as she slid into a chair.

"Thank you, Lydia," Grams said. "Maybe I can teach you how to make them while you're here."

"I'd sure like that," Lydia added.

Grams took the seat next to Pops, and they bowed their heads for the prayer.

After breakfast, Lydia and Grams were like racehorses raring to start, working with the fascinating items on the dining table.

"Slow down, girls." Pops said. "Let's work on the items from the wooden box first."

Lydia and Grams looked at each other and agreed.

Pops picked up his list and looked it over. "We know the furniture was made in Springfield, and Fannie Catts did the needlepoint work on the seat of the bench. She must have had the bench built as a place to hide valuables."

Pops looked thoughtfully at the items on the table. "Lydia, back in those times, people were always thinking of places to hide valuables from thieves. So, think about it—according to what Tate found, Fannie lived alone at the farm for twenty years after her grandmother, Frances Catts/Crawford died. Possibly, she had the vanity bench built like a piano bench with a concealed area and a lock. No one would think to look in a vanity bench. She had her own uniquely hidden lock box."

"That's really smart," Lydia said as she slid the container of items closer.

"Let me tell you what we know about Fannie Catts from our research with Tate last year," Grams said to Lydia. "Fannie came to Missouri in 1858 after she graduated from the Women's Academy in Wellsburg, Virginia. She wanted to become a schoolteacher here in Mount Vernon. We think she met a young man soon after she arrived. They fell in love and were engaged to be married."

"The first major battle of the Civil War west of the Mississippi River happened not far from our farm," Pops chimed in. "When word spread that the battle had started, Fannie's fiancé came by the farm to tell her goodbye. She watched as he rode away, but she never saw him again. She remained single the rest of her life.

"Also, Fannie's father, George Catts, set out to fight for the Union in the same battle. He was injured. His stepbrother, Colonel Robert Crawford, found him lying on the ground. He helped him onto a medical wagon going to Springfield. There he could receive medical attention.

"George later died not from his battle injuries but from typhoid fever, which weeks after the battle, contaminated the hospital. Fannie, as the oldest child, stayed at her mother's side to help with the other eight children."

"Eight brothers and sisters?" Lydia exclaimed. "Wow!" She didn't know anyone who had nine kids.

Grams smiled. "They had big families back then. Fannie's mother would've grieved deeply for her husband, George. She probably slipped into depression. Fannie may have helped her find strength in her faith."

Lydia placed the items back into the tapestry bag.

Grams laid the letters and other papers in the container and pushed it aside. "Like Pops said, those things might be a separate story," she added.

Unfolding the floor plan on the table, Pops looked at the details. He showed Lydia where the front door and other areas were located on the plan.

"This is amazing," Pops commented. "An 1885 original floor plan of our house—the house Fannie built. The drawing has a back porch that's no longer on our house. However, everything else looks the same."

"I forgot to show you something, Lydia," Pops said as he picked up a tiny cardboard folder of sewing needles. "I found this tucked in the corner of the bench. With it is a handwritten note that reads, 'Unlike Aunt Jane Ann and other women in my family, I never liked to sew. Determined, I finished my friendship quilt and the cushion on this bench. Whoever finds these needles, consider them a gift. I have sewed my last stitch. Fannie Catts."

Lydia admired Fannie's resolve to learn to do something she didn't like to do. The needlepoint cushion on the bench was splendid—her new favorite word. Fannie must have applied herself and studied hard to do something like this. Perhaps Grams was right. Maybe Lydia could learn to overcome her own problems and accomplish wonderful things.

They all laughed and headed to the kitchen for lunch.

 The rain continued in the afternoon, so Pops decided they would start with the items found in the wooden box. He handed Lydia one of the letters.

Unfolding the letter, she could see it was printed in big letters, so she began to read,

August 9, 1824

Dear Uncle John,

I am using the silver writing pen you gave me to write this letter. I hope I will be like you, a famous author or poet. I ask Mama to read your letters from London to me each night. Then I pray for you.

I have been sick with a fever for the last two days. I know I will be healthy when you return home for Christmas. I miss you so much.

"The letter seems to be unfinished. No one signed their name," Pops said.

Grams looked at the date then paged through the Catts/Crawford Bible. "Nine-year-old John Neal Catts died on that day from yellow fever. Oh, no! He never finished his letter to his uncle John Neal, Frances's brother."

Lydia took the writing pen from the black velvet bag. With a magnifying glass, she looked at it closely. Pops helped her find the words, *John Neal*, engraved on the side. He then showed her how it would've been used with an ink well.

The pen had been a gift from Frances's brother to his namesake nephew, John Neal.

While taking the pen from the bag, Lydia also found a note attached with a thread to the silver baby spoon.

Lydia had Grams help her read the note written on rose–colored paper, "This silver baby spoon with the initials C.C. was given to Charles Crawford from his brothers when he was born. Charles wanted the spoon given to little Clarence Catts, his nephew, since his initials were also C.C. After Clarence, and later Charles, dies, it is to be given to Jane Ann Catts Crawford who shares both family names.

"My heart continues to grieve for the family I never knew," Grams said as she reflected her thoughts toward all they had endured.

"Why did you say that, Grams?" Lydia asked.

"When I think of the stories we discovered when Tate was here last year … The Catts/Crawford family suffered so many losses of their family members. And through Frances's journal, I feel like I knew each one of them and learned to deeply care for them."

Lydia couldn't quite understand what she meant. How could someone know and love strangers? Still pondering what Grams said, she picked up another letter. As she took the faded yellow letter out of the envelope, a drawing of a lady and two little boys wearing derby hats slid out onto the table. She picked it up and turned it over. On the back was written, *Juanita Sammons and her sons, Willie and Pete.*

"May I read the letter to you?" Lydia asked, gaining confidence in her abilities to read aloud.

Grams smiled. "Sure, sweet Lydia."

Lydia began reading in a steady voice.

May 1, 1838

My dearest Mrs. Crawford,

I was told by travelers heading back east you are near a town called Springfield and are waiting for land to homestead. I promised I would write to you about Willie and Pete. They are now around nine and ten years old. Since we found no family papers after their parents and sisters drowned trying to cross the Mississippi River, I can only guess their ages. We celebrate both of their birthdays on February 8, the day you talked with me about taking the boys. That is the day my broken heart was healed by their sweet love.

We have been a family from that day forward. They have loved me and blessed me more than I can ever tell you. Willie has a servant's heart to help others. Perhaps he will become a preacher. Pete has an adventurous spirit. You might meet him one day as he travels west in pursuit of his dreams.

I thank God for Willie and Pete each day and for you, Mrs. Crawford, who brought me my sons.

I am forever thankful,

Juanita Sammons

Grams explained to Lydia the story of Willie and Pete's family. Sadly, their family drowned while crossing the Mississippi River. Frances Crawford took the boys to live with her until a permanent home could be found. She wrote in her journal that God found them a home on February 8, her birthday.

Pops picked up a folded card and helped Lydia read the scrolled, thick black letters inside. *Property of Charles Crawford.*

"He was the half-brother of both Jane Ann Catts and Robert Crawford. He took one thousand head of cattle from Sedalia, Missouri, to California. Soon after he arrived, Indians killed him," Pops told Lydia.

Reaching into the velvet bag, Pops pulled out a silver compass and held it up for Lydia to see. "It opens like a pocket watch," he said, showing her a tiny button that allowed the lid to spring open.

She picked up the magnifying glass and found the name *John Neal* on the back.

"Look here, Pops," she said. "On the leather strap is T. L. Catts. Did it belong to both of them?"

"Wait. Let me try to explain to you how family names were used over and over again," Pops said. "Frances Neal Catts Crawford's father came from England and was named John Neal. He named his son, John Neal II, who never had a son. Frances honored both her father and brother by naming her son John Neal Catts."

"If I remember the story correctly," Pops continued, looking up at the ceiling as he spoke, "the compass was passed from the Neal family to the Catts. Thomas L. loaned the compass to his brother, Charles, when he traveled west on a cattle drive. He teased his brother about wanting the compass back when he returned safely.

"Sadly, Charles didn't return, but instead died in California. When his partner, Daniel Fulbright, came home, he returned the compass to Thomas L, as Charles had requested."

Lydia rubbed her finger across the face of the compass. "Wow. This compass must have traveled many miles," she said, smiling. She put it down and reached over to pick up a tiny, silver cylindrical item. "What's this?"

Grams showed her how to slip it on her finger. "It's a thimble, which was used to push needles through thick cloth. Because women sewed so much, a thimble also protected their fingers from blisters. Jane Ann's mother taught her to sew and to make hats. The thimble most likely belonged to her mother or grandmother since there is an *N* engraved on it."

Lydia again reached into the black velvet bag, and this time handed Pops a silver pocket watch.

Pops leaned back in his chair and looked it over with the magnifying glass. Smiling, he said, "It has Thomas Crawford, Esq. on the back. This came from the Crawford side of the family."

The last item Lydia picked up was the blue broach, wrapped in a handkerchief which had the initials, *F. S. K.*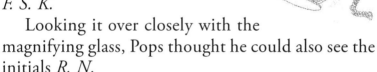

Looking it over closely with the magnifying glass, Pops thought he could also see the initials *R. N.*

 Grams searched through the list of names in the Catts/Crawford family Bible. "I assume it belonged to Frances's mother, Rachel Neal."

"But who was F. S. K.?" Lydia asked.

Grams and Pops sat back in their chair to think for a moment.

Then Grams looked up and smiled. "I think it was Francis Scott Key. Remember in Frances's journal, Pop? She attended his wedding when she was a little girl. She sneezed, and he gave her his handkerchief."

Lydia laughed as she carefully placed the items back into the velvet bag and laid them in the container. The last thing in the box was the thick, red-and-white threads. Lydia wondered what their special meaning might be.

Grams stood and laid the Bible on the table. As she did, a crocheted cross bookmarker fell from the Bible to the floor.

Lydia picked up the cross. Feeling a lump in the center, she turned the cross over and discovered a small key stitched to the back side.

"Another key!" Lydia excitedly said. She glanced around the table and picked up the diary. Rubbing the cracks in the worn old leather, she touched the letters which spelled, "Jane Ann." Still holding the cross in her hand, she inserted the key into the keyhole in the diary, turned it, and the diary lock popped open.

"The key is in God's Word!" Grams exclaimed. "That's where Jane Ann hid the key to her diary, stitched to the cross she put in God's Word."

Opening the diary, Lydia slowly read from the first page.

October 17, 1825

To my daughter, Jane Ann Catts

Happy Twelfth Birthday

Remember the Three Keys as you write your thoughts and prayers to God.

With love and prayers always,

Mama

"What were the three keys?" Lydia asked.

"They can't be the three we already found," Grams said. "Two were hidden by Fannie, and the diary key was hidden by Jane Ann."

Lydia turned the page. To her surprise, she could see the separation of each word. "This is amazing," she said. "I can read the words written by Jane Ann."

Grams smiled and gave Lydia a hug, thanking God for helping her be able to see the words more clearly.

GRAMMY BEAN'S CINNAMON ROLLS

Dough:
½ Cup melted butter
1 packet or 2 ¼ Tsp active dry yeast
2 Cups warm whole milk
1 tsp baking powder
½ Cup sugar
2 Tsp salt
5 Cups flour all-purpose flour
Filling
¾ Cup softened butter
2 Tbs ground cinnamon
¾ Cup light brown sugar
Frosting
4 oz. soft cream cheese
2 Tbs melted butter
2 Tbs half and half cream
2 tsp vanilla
1 Cup powdered sugar
Mix warm milk, butter, and sugar. Mixture needs to be warm (100-110°F).

Sprinkle yeast over the warm mixture and let stand for 1 minute.

Add 4 Cups all-purpose flour to milk mixture and mix. Cover and set in a warm place to rise for 1 hour.

Remove cover and add additional ¾ Cup flour baking powder salt.

Mix well and pour onto floured surface.

Roll and knead dough gently. Add more flour if needed until dough is smooth.

Roll dough out on a clean smooth counter or cutting board until ¾ inch thick.

Spread butter evenly over the dough. Sprinkle on brown sugar and cinnamon.

Roll dough to form a log. Tuck ends until smooth. Place seam-side down.

Slide dental floss under the bottom side of the log. Every 1½ inches, pull floss upward through the dough.

Place cinnamon rolls in a baking dish close together. Cover and place in a warm place to rise for 30 minutes. Preheat oven to 350°F.

Mix the frosting ingredients together until smooth.

Remove cover from dough and bake at 350 degrees for 25-30 minutes.

Remove from oven and spoon on frosting. Sprinkle with chopped pecans. When cooled serve with fresh raspberries or blackberries.

CHAPTER 3

America had taken huge leaps forward to secure its future as an independent nation, grounded in faith and ready to unleash its potential growth. After the Louisiana Purchase, President Jefferson established the Corps of Discovery and placed his friends, Captain Meriwether Lewis and Captain William Clark, in command to explore and create maps of the new territory. Known as the Lewis and Clark Expedition, they left Saint Louis, Missouri, on May 14, 1804 and returned to Saint Louis on September 25, 1806, with maps showing their eight-thousand-mile adventure.

Their mapping expedition revealed trails that would expand America all the way to the Pacific Ocean. Many people with an adventurous spirit followed their trails westward bound.

Among those with dreams to go west was the Catts/Crawford family. They stepped out in faith to be counted as American Pioneers.

THE STORY OF JANE ANN CATTS/CRAWFORD

Born Oct. 17th, 1813 to Frances (Neal) Catts/Crawford and John M. Catts

Lydia could hardly contain herself as she continued reading in Jane Ann Catts's diary.

October 17, 1825

Today is my birthday. I am twelve years old. Mama gave me this diary so I can write my thoughts and prayers. Writing is much easier for me than reading.

My brothers surprised me with a new invention. It is called a balloon. They blew air into a red flat circle making it grow bigger and bigger. They tied it to a string for me to carry around. To surprise Mama, they blew up a yellow balloon and placed it under the cushion of her chair. When she sat on it, "Boom," it popped. She laughed out loud for the first time since Papa died.

I will never stop missing my Papa or my brother, John Neal.

Jane Ann Catts was only five years old when her father, John M. Catts, died in 1818. Her brother, George, was six, John Neal was not yet three, and her youngest brother, Thomas L, was two months old.

Her mother, a young, grieving widow at age twenty-six, was left with four children to raise on her own.

With no money to support her family, she did what her mother taught her. Frances found the silver thimble that belonged to her mother, began creating beautiful hats, and sold them to the society women of Baltimore. Eventually, she owned a successful hat shop on Lexington Avenue. The Catts family lived above the hat shop in an apartment with a big window which looked down on the busy streets of Baltimore.

To add to the family's heartache, young John Neal Catts, age nine, suddenly died of yellow fever.

Christmas 1825

I am making a special Christmas gift for Mama. Her heart is still broken about John Neal and Papa. She sits by the fire in the hearth room crying most every night. I gathered scrap fabric to make her a quilt. My sewing is not as nice as Mama's, but I am learning. As I sewed each piece together, I prayed for her.

The Catts family holiday traditions included the children waking up on holiday mornings to find Sweet Milk Sugar Cookies under their pillows— an English tradition started generations before in London. On this Christmas Eve, Jane Ann woke up when her mother put the cookies under her pillow. She lay awake for a long time, listening to her mother cry. With a compassionate heart, she took the quilt she made and wrapped it around her mother's shoulders. Perhaps the quilt opened her mama's heart to feel the love and comfort of God she desperately needed. The empty spot in her heart had been filled by Jane Ann's love.

Grams glanced at Lydia and said, "I'll be right back."

When she returned, she held up a quilt Lydia had made for her last Christmas. Draping it over Lydia's shoulders, Grams said, "You filled my heart with love too."

February 1826

I can write letters and spell most words, but when I try to read, the letters jumble together. I memorize as many words as I can, but sometimes I have to stare at the words until they separate. Then I can see each word clearly. I will keep working on my reading until I can read as well as my brothers.

Two birthday gifts are hidden under my bed. For Mama I made a pink hat with roses. For my brother George, who I think considers himself to be the man in the family, I made a bag to keep his rocks in for his slingshot. He goes out into the side alley and practices hitting targets. I confessed to George that I sometime feel afraid without Papa in the house to protect us. He assured me between the wooden stick he keeps beside his bed and his slingshot, he can defend our family. I am thankful for his efforts.

Baltimore was the largest and fastest growing port city in America. With the growth, came criminals and crime. Hearing ladies in the hat shop talk about the increase in crime made Jane Ann fearful.

Late one evening, she heard her mother tell one of the ladies about the night when evil roamed the streets of Baltimore. She said she was a young girl when the scary night happened and the feeling of fear continues to haunt her even as an adult.

She said her father arrived home early one evening and locked the doors, telling everyone to stay inside and stay away from the windows. Without a word, he found his pistol and slipped it in the side pocket of his jacket.

Her mother blew out the oil lamps and quickly gathered the children around the flickering fireplace, the only light in the dark room. They held their children close and whispered prayers all night while listening to every scary sound echoing from the streets below. The next morning they heard what had happened.

Baltimore's first small police force, called Night Watchmen, was organized in 1784. Unfortunately, their first casualty was a police officer who was killed on March 15, 1808. Nine chain-gang prisoners escaped from the Baltimore City Jail by using pewter eating utensils they hammered into make-shift keys to unlock their cells. They also made a three-inch knife which they used to stab officer N.W. George Workner. He died the following day. All nine violent criminals were recaptured and convicted of the crime. Four were hanged and five were given a life sentence.

Officer Workner was America's first law enforcement officer killed in the line of duty.

Jane Ann never told her mother she heard her telling the story. She kept her untold fear to herself so not to scare her brothers.

JUST A MOMENT

July 4, 1826

With my pen, I write the letters in my diary, "Happy Fiftieth Birthday to America." This is a day I cannot wait to celebrate. I love the excitement of the parade, picnic, and beautiful bursting fireworks at Fort McHenry. I am taught to be thankful for our freedom and for those, like my father, who served to protect us. I hope we never forget not one single soldier who serves our country. And I pray God will never lift his hand of blessing from America.

October 17, 1826

I am thirteen years old today. Since my reading is improving, I will be allowed to take the day off from my studies. While I wait for my mother and brothers to finish their work, I will sit by our big window, dreaming, as I gaze at the world below.

I notice prissy Mrs. Greene's big gaudy hat is a resting place for drifting fall leaves. She will never notice them among the many ribbons and flowers on her hat.

I watch Thomas's friends playing kick the can in the side alley, and I see some street boys sneaking behind a fence to smoke a cigar. They look like they are choking more than they are smoking.

I also see my friend Bradley helping an older lady up the steps to her house while Pastor Marshall at Old Otterbein Church serves food to the needy.

I wonder if people watch me. If they do, what will they see? I hope it is the joy that Mama teaches us about.

J – Jesus first.

O – Others second.

Y – Yourself last.

From a young age, Jane Ann's parents taught her to think of others before herself. The joy her mother talked about was something she would use the rest of her life. She realized it was a daily choice she would need to make.

"Lydia," Grams said, looking over at her granddaughter. "Like Jane Ann was taught, choosing joy is something we do each day. It fills our heart with an unexplainable feeling of happiness. It has taken me a lifetime to learn that my life is not about me, but instead it's what God wants me to do with my life."

She could tell Lydia was pondering the acronym meaning of the JOY.

November 1826

Mama received a letter from our long-time family friend, Thomas Crawford, telling her he was bringing his sick wife to Baltimore to visit a doctor. Always doing for others, Mama packed a basket of food, and when we delivered it to their family, we met his four sons.

The Catts children were taught by example to help others. Jane Ann had a soft, compassionate heart. To help her memorize Scriptures about helping others, her mother showed her how to insert her name into Bible verses.

"Let all your things, Jane Ann, be done in charity," (I Corinthians 16:14)

Jane Ann's father served in the war with Mr. Crawford. He was a respected lawyer and a gentlemen apple farmer from Wellsburg, Virginia. Frances's compassion for his sick wife perhaps bonded their friendship.

Lydia reached for a pencil and paper to write the Scripture, "Let all your things, Lydia, be done in charity."

"Charity, in this case, means love," Grams explained. "I used to write my name in Scriptures like Jane Ann did and now you're doing it."

Spring 1827

Mama received a card from Thomas Crawford telling her his wife had passed away. Remembering how kind she was saddened my heart. I went to my room and cried, thinking how much it would hurt if Mama died. I still sometimes cry when I miss my Papa and John Neal. I asked God to please keep Mama strong and able to stay with us for always. I pray for the Crawford boys who will also miss their Mama.

Frances and her children wrote a note to the Crawford Family expressing their sympathy at the death of Mrs. Crawford. Memories of their own loss perhaps bonded the families together. Both families felt compassion for one another.

May 1828

My window is open, and the smell of lavender fills my room. The corner street vendors have many different kinds of spring flowers, but my favorite will always be lavender and lilac. When I was a little girl, I remember my Papa bringing Mama lavender flowers and calling her his Lavender Lady.

Yesterday, Mr. Crawford and his sons visited with us while he was in Baltimore on business. Our families enjoy time together. I noticed Mama and Mr. Crawford liked one another. I think they are falling in love. My heart sings to see a season of happiness for Mama. Mr. Crawford brought her a bouquet of lavender flowers. Perhaps it is God's way of letting me know Papa would approve.

Jane Ann's mother had been a widow for over ten years. She devoted her life to her children after John Catts died. Thomas Crawford, a widow for over a year, wanted someone else in his life. Since the families had known each other for many years, it seemed natural for them to be together. However, it would be a season of change for everyone.

> To everything there is a season, and
> a time to every purpose under the
> heaven:
>
> A time to be born and a time to die;
>
> a time to plant, and a time to pluck

up that which is planted;

A time to kill, and a time to heal;

a time to break down, and a time to build up;

A time to weep, and a time to laugh;

a time to mourn, and a time to dance;

A time to cast away stones, and a time to gather stones together;

a time to embrace, and a time to refrain from embracing;

A time to get, and a time to lose;

a time to keep, and a time to cast away;

A time to rend, and a time to sew;

a time to keep silence, and a time to speak;

A time to love, and a time to hate;

a time of war, and a time of peace.

(Ecclesiastes 3:1-8 KJV)

Christmas 1828

I again sit by the big window in our hearth room looking down upon the busy streets of the city. I have so many memories of sitting by this window, watching the snow fall and pile up in the corners on the ledge. I watch as the frosty ice forms on the windows like shattered crystals. And I laugh when I think of the many snowball fights I watched my brothers have in the alley.

I close my eyes and hear the carolers on the corner singing Christmas Carols to raise money for the poor, and oh how I love the sound of the bells at the Old Otterbein Church. So many memories I hold dear in my heart.

I open my eyes to see a surprise. Mr. Crawford and his sons are waving to me from a beautiful, red, horse-drawn sleigh on the street below. Robert, his son, suggested his father take us all for a ride. Mama handed George, Thomas, and me our coats, hats, and mittens. Out the door we ran for a sleigh ride in the fresh snow.

The big window had special memories for Jane Ann and her mother. She remembered stories her mother, Frances, told her about watching from the big window as her father marched away to war. She waved to him until she could see him no more and then fell to her knees to pray. She watched young men who couldn't read or write, stand in line to make their "X" as a way to sign their names to become patriot soldiers during the War of 1812. As much as she didn't like to talk about the war, she also didn't want her children to forget the price others paid for their freedom. So many memories are tucked away in their minds.

While sitting by the fire on Christmas Eve, Frances told Jane Ann about a Christmas letter she once received from her father. On the corner of his letter was a drawing of a country church. He wrote about his soldiers taking refuge in an abandoned church on Christmas Eve. They were unable to build a fire in fear their enemies would notice the smoke. So, they huddled inside to stay warm.

Neighboring families received word the American soldiers had taken shelter. They gathered blankets and food to deliver all they had to the soldiers in the church. The families entered through the back door of the church softly singing, "Silent Night, Holy Night."

Sitting by the fire, Frances told Jane Ann about her dear friend, Francis Scott Key, who wrote a poem which became the song, "The Star-Spangled Banner."

She often showed Jane Ann the piece of the American flag from Fort McHenry and the sign her father, John Catts, carved during his illness as her Christmas gift. The precious words, *In God Is Our Trust*, gave Frances hope.

Before long, Thomas Crawford and Frances Catts had fallen in love. Perhaps, the sleigh ride is where the two families started new memories together. And in time, they would be able to tuck their sad memories away in their mind.

Early Spring1829

Easter hats and Easter bonnets are in high demand. Mama has agreed to let me help her in the hat shop. I work hard on my reading at night, and I rise early to do my other studies so I can hurry downstairs to the hat shop just as the bell rings for our first customer. I am learning many of Mama's fancy stitches that make her hat designs so unique.

Today, she allowed me to make my first hat by myself. She even let me use some of her special glass buttons she hides away in a blue velvet box. Oh, how I love to sew, and I have so many ideas in my mind just waiting for me to create.

This morning, Mama told us we have been invited to visit the Crawford family at their home in Wellsburg. I do believe love is in their hearts.

The Catts Fine Millenary Shop was the place to find stylish spring hats. In ladies' social circles, it became known as the finest hat shop in Baltimore.

However, Jane Ann saw her mother gradually letting go of the responsibilities with the hat shop. She loved that she was finally finding happiness in a new direction. Rachel, Frances's sister, had shown interest in buying the shop if Frances should ever want to sell.

The Crawford and Catts families meshed together quickly. Thomas asked Frances to marry him and move to Wellsburg. The Catts family accepts the proposal of the Crawford family. Jointly, they declared they will be known as the Catts/Crawford Family.

The most difficult part of the move would be saying goodbye to Rachel, John Neal, and Frances's beloved friend, Francis Scott Key. And for them to leave behind the graves of the ones they loved.

JUST A MOMENT

June 1829

Mama's wedding was perfect. She and Papa, as I will now call him, overflowed with love for each other. I have never seen her so happy. Our four new brothers joined hands with George, Thomas, and me to become one family — the Catts/Crawford family.

I will soon begin school at the Girl's Academy in Wellsburg. I do not know anyone and am afraid I will be made fun of because I read more slowly. I am thankful Papa wants to walk me to school and introduce me as his new daughter. He grew up in Wellsburg and knows most of the families.

After breakfast, I watched George and Thomas L, as we now called him, go with the Crawford boys for their first day of school. They ran across the green meadow, climbed a white fence, and walked to the home of Alexander Campbell where they will do their studies in Greek and Latin

Since Papa's name is Thomas, we have all agreed to call my brother, Thomas Love Catts, Thomas L.

Changes and a new life are ahead for all of us. My only complaint is the smell of six brothers is difficult at times.

FRANCES CATTS/CRAWFORD'S SWEET MILK SUGAR COOKIES

1 Cup butter
2 Cups sugar
¼ Cup whole milk
Heat the above ingredients in saucepan on low heat for five minutes or until sugar is completely dissolved. Stir constantly with a whisk. Do not let boil.

Cool for five minutes.
Add:
1 beaten egg
2 Tbs real vanilla
Add vanilla to egg and beat gently. Slowly add to the butter, sugar, and milk. Set aside.

Sift or dry whisk together the following ingredients:
5 Cups plain flour
1 ½ tsp baking powder
½ tsp baking soda
¼ tsp salt
¼ tsp cinnamon
Add to first mixture a little at a time to the dry ingredients until dough is formed. Add flour if needed.

Roll into three balls and place in a glass bowl covered. Use quickly as the dough doesn't last long.

Pre-heat oven to 350 degrees.

Lay out wax paper or use a clean countertop to roll out cookie dough. Sprinkle flour on surface and pat out cookie dough. Sprinkled top with flour. Roll dough out to ¼ inch thick. Use a large glass or cookie cutter to cut cookies. Place on ungreased cookie sheet.

Leave plenty of space between cookies. Sprinkle the top of cookies with white or colored sugar if desired.

Bake at 350 degrees for 7 to 8 minutes. Lay out on wax paper or cooling rack to cool.

Ice cookies if desired

Icing:
2 ½ Cups powdered sugar
3 Tbs of butter, softened
2 Tsp of vanilla
1 Tbs sweet milk

This was a tradition that started in London generations before the Catts/Crawford family came to America. Cookies were wrapped and put under the children's pillow for each holiday.

CHAPTER 4

A new life began for Jane Ann. She was now a sister to six rambunctious brothers. Being out numbered had some good advantages. Soft-hearted Papa most often took her side in disagreements.

To teach six boys and one girl to get along, Thomas had them pick apples together. Long hours side by side working in the orchards and throwing rotten apples eventually worked. They adjusted to being a family. It took time, but they were finally the Catts/Crawford family.

October 17, 1829

Today is my sixteenth birthday, and I am now a woman. Just a moment changed my life. I have been called a child far too long. I am like a caterpillar anxiously waiting to change into a butterfly. Today I feel as though I could spread my wings and fly away. But for now, I guess I will go help Mama in the kitchen.

Dear Lord,

I want to experience the world you created. Open the eyes of my heart to see what others pass by. Guide me to my wonderful future.

Jane Ann wanted to grow up. She dreamed about the man she would fall in love with one day. Little did she know how close her true love might be.

JUST A MOMENT

Christmas 1829

This, our first Christmas together, has been yet another adjustment. The Crawford family has just as many traditions as our family. We are learning from one another. I helped Mama make our traditional Sweet-Milk Sugar Cookies which she will place under everyone's pillow to find on Christmas morning. After attending the Christmas Eve candlelight service at church, we shared our first Christmas dinner as a family. Afterward, Papa had us gather around the fireplace. This was the first time I heard the story about the Bethlehem Star in the center of an apple.

Papa stood in front of the dancing, glowing fire to tell us the story. He picked up an apple and cut it sideways with a knife. He held up the apple, and for the first time I could see the star in the middle surrounding the seeds. Amazed, I listened as he told us how God created all things perfect until sin entered the world. God knew he had to provide a way to bring us back to him. So, he sent his only son Jesus, who was born in the town of Bethlehem in Israel.

That night a beautiful star shinned brightly in the sky to let the world know where their Savior would be born. I listened as Papa told us again God's ways are perfect. In the center of every apple he has placed a star to remind us of the Bethlehem Star and the night Jesus was born. He handed me one of the apple seeds and let me touch the star. He explained we can count the seeds in an apple, but only God knows how many apples are in each seed.

I will never forget this moment. I realized I needed a Savior and his name is Jesus.

After Thomas Crawford shared the story about the Bethlehem star, he read from the family Bible in Luke 2 about the night Jesus was born. Their first Christmas as the Catts/Crawford family was just as God had planned. Perfect.

"Grams," Lydia softly said, "I have asked Jesus into my heart. Mom and Dad prayed with me as I asked Jesus to forgive me of my sins and to please come to live in my heart forever."

Grams hugged Lydia tightly and said, "Jesus loves you forever, and so do I."

Early summer 1830

I am so happy for Mama and Papa. She is going to have a baby. God's gift of a Catts/Crawford baby will bring new joy into our hearts. Thomas L will finally be a big brother to someone. I might have a little sister. I have never seen Mama so excited. She thinks the baby will arrive in February.

It was a perfect time for Frances and Thomas to make their announcement. On their first wedding anniversary, after a celebration supper, Thomas asked everyone to remain at the table. He handed a piece of paper to their six boys and gave Jane Ann the last piece of paper. He asked them one by one to read the word on their paper. Robert started and his brothers followed.

"We ..."

"Are ..."

"Going …"
"To …"
"Have …"
"A …"
"Baby!" Jane Ann squealed. Excitement filled the Catts/Crawford house like never before.

Jane Ann was sad to think Robert would be gone for so long. He made the decision, with the endorsement of his Uncle Charles Hammond, to attend West Point Military Academy. He was required to make the commitment to stay for two years with no leave to come home.

February 14, 1831

Mama had everything ready. Even the Sweet-Milk Sugar Cookies were wrapped for Valentine's Day. She seemed fine when we left for church. When she grabbed Papa's hand and squeezed it tightly during the offertory prayer, he knew the time had come. Halfway through Pastor Gilmore's sermon, our entire family stood and marched out of the church. I think everyone could tell Mama was on her way home to have a baby. Papa was glad his sister, Aunt Cokey as she was called, was there to help.

It seemed like I could hear Mama moaning in pain for a long time. And then we heard the baby cry. Papa rushed in to be with Mama. Soon he walked out with our little brother, Charles Catts/Crawford, in his arms.

Even though Jane Ann hoped for a baby sister, never could a baby be more loved. She was her mother's right hand in helping care for baby Charles.

Fall 1831

I think Mama is in shock. It was not as if I was trying to listen to their conversation. I would never do that. All the windows in the house are open, letting the cool fall breeze flow through the house before winter. I was reading a book as I do every afternoon after school when my chores are finished. As I enjoyed my time on the porch swing, Papa came in to sit with Mama while she nursed baby Charles. He told her he has been thinking we should go west to homestead land. I did not hear her utter a word. Last week some of our neighbors came by to tell us goodbye. They are going to Missouri in a covered wagon and will let Papa know where they settle. I hope that will not be our family anytime soon. For now, I will leave that worry at the foot of my bed where I pray each night. And maybe it will be gone by morning.

After the Louisiana Purchase was signed, thousands of acres of land had to be settled and occupied all the way to the Pacific Ocean. Those willing to cross the mighty Mississippi River and follow the sun west, would be known as American pioneers. Each family willing to step out in faith to go west would have the opportunity to homestead one-hundred, sixty acres of land.

When Jane Ann accidentally heard her parents' conversation, just like a planting a seed starts an apple tree, the idea to go west was planted. Thomas knew he had to wait for the idea to take root with Frances. Perhaps, it was his adventurous spirit or his desire to make his mark in history that fueled his dream to go west. Whatever his reason, he'd started the discussion, hoping Frances would take his hand and step out in faith with him.

Spring 1832

Once again, I am in my favorite place, writing in my diary. The white swing with the squeak in the chain is where I go to find myself. Mama asked me to keep an eye on baby Charles while she and Papa check the blooms on the apple trees. He thinks perhaps some were nipped by a late frost.

I watch baby Charles toddle around the yard, searching for Thomas L. They are playing hide and go seek among the maple trees. My brother is like corn in the field, very tall so Charles easily finds him. Watching them play and listening to their laughter, I understand why it is such a difficult decision for Mama. I watch her and Papa walking hand in hand in the apple orchard. I am concerned their conversation is not going well. Mama turned and walked away from Papa. He quickly caught up to her and hugged her close. I think he is wiping away her tears. They are now walking back to the house with their arms around one another. It takes time for a seed to grow.

Earlier today I saw Papa give Thomas L his father's apple-seed box with the cross-cut apple carved on the top. I watched my brother's face light up with a smile. He is perhaps honored to receive the treasured family keepsake.

I receive a letter from Robert at least once a month. His two-year commitment at West Point will soon be finished, and he will come home. I cannot imagine how handsome and grown up he must be. I hope he does not think I am still a child. I cannot wait to see him.

*As I swing back and forth, looking at this beautiful place
we are privileged to call home, I think about the many
sacrifices that are ahead. So many unknowns I can't begin
to imagine.*

"Why would they want to move from that
wonderful farm, Grams?" Lydia asked. "I can't
imagine you and Pops moving away from the farm."

"The opportunity to go west was exciting to
everyone back then," Grams answered. "The chance
at starting a new life on new land appealed to many
people. But husbands and wives had to seriously
consider the sacrifices and the dangers their family
might face. The government offered one-hundred
and sixty acres of free land to families willing to make
the sacrifices to become American pioneers. The west
had to be dotted with settlers in order for America
to continue the growth it needed for the future."

"What did they sacrifice, Grams?" Lydia asked.

"A sacrifice is something you give up to make
someone else happy or to accomplish something for
the good of all people. Pioneers left their family
and homes to move west. If they hadn't gone west,
the Fulton farm may not have been homesteaded
or all the land between here and California. They
sacrificed for the good of future generations," Grams
explained.

Lydia thought about what Grams said. It never
occurred to her that someone would sacrifice

something for people in the future that they would never know

"It's been a long day of reading," Grams said. "Let's get ready for bed. We'll have to come back to this tomorrow."

"This is more fun than I ever expected," she replied. "Tomorrow, we can take turns reading the diary again."

"And maybe we can finish sanding and oiling the furniture so it's ready for you to take home," Pops chimed into the conversation.

They said their goodnights, and Lydia tucked herself into bed. She lay still for a long time listening to the hoot owls calling back and forth to each other in the nearby woods. Unable to sleep, she thought about how well Grams could read from Jane Ann's diary. She wondered if she too would be able to improve her reading if she kept working at it.

Talking about her Dyslexia with Grams encouraged Lydia. Instead of being afraid of reading, she liked the challenge of reading more in Jane Ann's diary.

With Wooster snoring on the rug beside her bed, Lydia fell asleep with a thankful heart to be at the farm with Grams and Pops.

The next morning, she arose feeling refreshed and ready to go. After breakfast, she went to get the diary and met Grams and Pops on the front porch. They took turns reading and sanding on the furniture while it continued to rain. Grams helped her with difficult words and encouraged her to memorize the words by sight to make her reading easier.

When the rain slowed, the robins and wrens called out in song to each other to welcome glimpses of sunshine before the next downpour of rain. The porch was just as Pops thought, a perfect place to work.

Early summer 1832

More families are leaving behind what is familiar and heading west to the unknown. Every wagon Papa watches rolling down the main road going west stirs his heart of adventure. For Mama, he is asking a lot for her to again give up everything she loves to follow his dream. My brothers who are old enough will need to decide if they want to stay behind to keep the apple farm or go west. When Mama, George, Thomas L, and I left Baltimore, none of us looked back. With excitement, we faced our future. This time it will be more difficult. Many more walks in the apple orchards will need to be taken before final decisions are made.

The number of west-bound wagons increased. They were filled with the hopes and dreams of families that wanted a stake in the rich fertile land west of the Mississippi River. Some rushed to pack up what little they had and grabbed hold of the promise for a better future. Together the Catts/Crawford family prayed for many months before making their decision.

Late August 1832

I try not to think about how excited I am to see Robert.

JUST A MOMENT

I keep reminding myself he is my stepbrother. After two years of writing to one another, my heart seems to think of him differently. Through our letters we have grown to know one another. He has shared his dreams to become a lawyer and to have a family. With every letter I feel closer to Robert. I'm uncertain what love feels like, but I know my heart feels differently toward him. Everyone is ready for his homecoming party tonight. I made a new blue dress, his favorite color. I sit on the porch waiting for him. I wait to see his handsome face as he rides across the green grassy meadow.

Robert rode up like a knight in shining armor on a beautiful black stallion just as Jane Ann had expected. She anxiously awaited his arrival with the whole family. As everyone stepped out to welcome him home, she stood on the porch, waiting for him to notice her. When his eyes met hers, they both knew their feelings had changed into something more than stepbrother and sister.

Even Uncle Charles Hammond, a judge from Cincinnati who attended the party, noticed Robert and Jane Ann's attraction to each other.

The evening after Robert's welcome-home party, Jane Ann helped her mother prepare an exceptional meal for the family. After they finished eating, they continued their conversation around the huge harvest table. As their talk quieted down, everyone stared at their plates, perhaps pondering their future.

Frances broke the silence by announcing she wanted to go west.

"So, if pioneers would move west, America would grow bigger?" Lydia asked.

"Yes, with every wagon that rolled west, it carried people to build new towns," Grams explained. "New towns meant communities to build schools, churches, and new business. Towns eventually would grow into cities with more schools and churches and even bigger business where people could raise their families and have jobs."

"I understand how our towns and cities were built," Lydia said. "But it's so hard to imagine families who didn't know where they were going or how long it would take them to get there."

"I can't either," Grams said. "They stepped out in faith that God would take them where he wanted them to go. They placed their hope and trust in him to take care of them."

Christmas 1834

Everyone is home for Christmas. I helped Mama make the extra-big cookies to place under everyone's pillow. I can tell she is sad that tonight will be our last Christmas supper together. She is making everyone's favorite foods and writing down her recipes to leave with my brothers who will stay in Virginia.

Perhaps it is the reality of our last Christmas together that caused everyone to be quiet during our meal. Or maybe they were thinking about the many changes that will occur in the near future.

After supper, Papa called us over to sit by the warm, hickory fire. As is our family tradition, he cut the apple to tell the story about the Bethlehem Star and to read the Christmas story.

After we sang "Silent Night," little Charles started tapping his foot and handed Thomas L his fiddle.

Robert took my hand and Papa took Mamas. Laughing and singing, we danced around and around the room. Robert handed me my shawl and asked if I would like to go out on the porch to watch it snow. We sat snuggled together on the porch swing, watching the silent snow fall.

Suddenly he whispered into my ear, "I love you, Jane Ann."

Words I had waited so long to hear.

Then he asked me to marry him. The question I had waited so long to answer. Yes!

Just as everyone had suspected, Jane Ann and Robert were in love. George knew it was just a matter of time before his stepbrother would propose to his sister.

Their last Christmas Eve together started with sadness but ended with music, dancing, and laughter. The evening was topped off with a wedding announcement. No one ever forgot their last Christmas together in Virginia.

Now that the decision had been made to go west, the family had many other plans they needed to make together. The time to go west would depend on when Robert and Jane Ann wanted to be married. They thought perhaps a fall wedding would give their parents time to properly prepare provisions and still allow time to cross the Mississippi River before winter. Robert and Jane Ann decided he would read law with his Uncle Charles Hammond in Cincinnati for two years before he and Jane Ann go west.

Most people never understood the heart of someone who would willingly choose to leave everything behind to become an American pioneer. Not only the men had the courage but even more so the women and children. Their choice meant probably never seeing those they love ever again, as well as facing the hardships of rugged travel and unforeseen death of those they loved. The decision was both exciting and challenging for a family.

Summer 1834

My beautiful wedding dress is finished. I am ready to marry my beloved Robert. We have decided to be married across the Ohio River in Steubenville at his mother's sister's house. As our wedding gift, she has offered her beautiful garden and home for the ceremony. And a week in the little cabin her father built when they settled in Ohio as a honeymoon cottage.

Robert has crossed the Ohio River many times on Martin's Ferry, but it will be my first time. I try not to think about how difficult travel will be for us in the coming days, only that I will be with the man I love.

JUST A MOMENT

Mama has given me the Catts family wedding trunk filled with china, silver, and other family treasures. I am thankful our family will be together for the wedding.

Robert and I will leave from the wedding for our honeymoon and then begin our journey in our own wagon on to Cincinnati. Uncle Charles has opened his home for us to stay with him. Robert will work part-time for him while he reads law. Mama and Papa will leave after the wedding and wait for us in Cincinnati where they will have a long visit with Uncle Charles before they go on west to Missouri.

I find it humorous that Mama and I will become pioneer women at the same time, at least until we reach Cincinnati. I cannot bear to think of leaving my brother George behind in Virginia or saying goodbye to my Crawford brothers. George, Thomas L, and I depended on each other after Papa died and felt we needed to take care of Mama. Now, the time has come for us to each decide our own future.

Other than the excitement of our wedding, everyone is silent about the changes we know are coming. For some, their silence echoes their love for each other while others grasp for moments of time together.

The sound of the back-door closing woke me up last night. I looked out the kitchen window and saw Mama and Papa standing under the arbor in the garden where they were married. The summer blue hydrangeas were still in bloom. In the soft moonlight, they stood holding one another. Mama pressed her head against Papa's shoulder, and I could see the glistening tears on her cheeks.

I went back to bed and cried myself to sleep. Every moment seems to be changing our life and taking us in different directions. I choose to hold on to the words my father carved when I was just a child. Robert and I will build the foundation of our marriage upon those words. "In God is our trust."

As the family prepared for the wedding, their excitement grew. At the same time, everyone's feelings of sadness weren't discussed. As each day passed, the reality of the family no longer being together was on the minds and hearts of everyone. Jane Ann, George, and Thomas L sat on the porch for hours sharing memories about their father and growing up in Baltimore.

Robert and George walked down to Wheeling Creek to skip rocks one last time and to remember when they cut their fingers, rubbed their blood together, and promise to be blood brothers forever.

Frances took little Charles for long walks around the home place, hoping to imprint memories in his mind of his first home.

Thomas spent hours with his sons walking through the apple orchards where they shared family memories. He walked with his four sons one last time to their mother's grave to lay flowers. And he walked through each room of the house that he and his father built, where his sons were born, and where his wife, Helen, died.

Each person had to take their last walk down memory lane before stepping into their future.

Unknown to Frances, Thomas had attached the sign, "In God is our trust," to the footboard of their wagon.

Each time they stepped up on their wagon, they would place their feet firmly on those words. And wherever their journey took them, they would step down with confidence in the hope and trust they placed in God.

CHAPTER 5

September 15, 1834

I was awake before sunrise, praying for Robert and myself. The love chapter in God's Word kept flowing through my mind. I remember Mama's dear friend, Ms. Ruth, who had her own way of saying I Corinthians 13.

In her humble sweet spirit, she would say,

"I don't want to be jealous, boastful, proud, or rude. I don't want to be irritable nor keep a record of being wronged. I don't want to rejoice at injustice. I want to be patient and kind and to rejoice when truth wins. I want to never give up, never lose faith, always be hopeful and endure every circumstance. I want to be a woman of faith and hope, but mostly a woman of love."

I want to be a woman of great wisdom like Mama's friend, Mrs. Ruth.

I am glad to leave behind the gossip of the ladies in town. They have whispered their opinion of Robert and me getting married for months. Papa tells me he is proud to give me, his only stepdaughter, away to his son. In just a short time, Papa will walk me down the garden path, place my hand in Robert's hand, and bestow upon us his blessings. This is the day my dreams will finally come true; I will marry the man I love. The moment I declare, "I do," my life will change forever. And I pray the gossipy ladies will NOT find someone else to talk about.

A carpet of red, gold, and orange leaves was gently laid down by the hand of God for Robert and Jane Ann. They stood under an arch created with yellow and white mums. The warm sun shined from heaven as the couple said their vows. The Catts/Crawford Family gathered around the newlyweds to ask God to bless, protect, and guide them.

After their wedding party, Jane Ann and Robert said their bittersweet goodbyes to family and friends—some they would never see again. Jane Ann held tightly to her brother, George, as they said their final goodbye.

He and Thomas L tied a white bow and cans to the back of the wagon. Thomas L lifted little Charles up to hang a bell on the neck of their horse. Jane Ann and Robert began the adventure of their life with a shower of rice falling on the path God had laid before them.

September 22, 1834

Our first week of marriage was all I dreamed it would be. Robert was kind and caring, and he pampered me each morning with breakfast in bed. We left the world for someone else to worry about for our week alone in the cabin.

Unfortunately, we did have another family at the cabin with us. A mama skunk and her kittens made their home under the porch. The bright harvest moonlight allowed us to watch from the window as the kittens followed mama along the creek behind the cabin and into the woods. With every step, she taught them how to dig for grub worms and bugs. Unfortunately, from the open window, we could smell them when they returned home.

Tomorrow, we are on our way to Cincinnati. With Mama's recommendations, we will purchase food and supplies before leaving Steubenville. Neither Robert nor I have ever traveled by covered wagon. As long as we are together, we are happy.

Jane Ann and Robert didn't think about the challenges they'd meet at every corner before reaching Cincinnati. Their young, innocent love blinded them as to what was ahead. Travelers going west offered to allow them to travel along with them for safety, but Robert and Jane Ann graciously declined. They wanted time alone.

September 24, 1834

I never imagined I would rather walk than ride in the wagon. The trail most traveled to Cincinnati was washed out by late spring rains. The only alternate trail we can find takes us miles out of our way. The roughness of the trail less traveled is over high rolling hills covered with shallow rocky soil.

My first night cooking on an open fire was frightening. I caught the bottom edge of my dress on fire. I was thankful Robert threw water all over me. I burned the salt pork and beans so badly, I had to scrape them from the bottom of the iron skillet. With not a word of complaint, my kindhearted husband pitched his burnt biscuits into the woods for the animals.

Up early the next morning, I hurried off to the woods. Along the way, I passed the biscuits even the animals would not eat. So many thoughts of doubt enter my mind. I search my heart for a Scripture to slow down my whirlwind of insecurities. I repeat what King David wrote in Psalms, "When I am afraid, I will trust in You."

Jane Ann and Robert started their marriage by attempting the impossible. She was raised in the city, and he was a well-educated apple farmer. After the first few days of travel in a covered wagon, perhaps they thought traveling with their parents might not have been a bad idea. Just as all newlyweds do, they experienced the good, the bad, and the unknown together as one.

September 26, 1834

Every day is a new challenge. I have learned to read a map and can tell approximate time by the sun. Robert is learning to watch for snakes as he gathers firewood. We were warned by a man on horseback to watch for nests of baby copperhead snakes that are plentiful in the woods this time of year. He advised us that no matter how small a copperhead snake is, it is still poisonous.

We stopped early in the afternoon to camp beside a clean, spring-water creek. We played like kids in the creek before taking a bath with our clothes on. While we bathed and washed our clothes with a bar of soap. We changed into dry clothes and hug our wet ones to dry by the fire.

We were laughing about our new way of bathing when I looked up and saw a native Indian step out from behind a tree. I was so frightened I could not speak. Robert slowly walked toward him, but he was suddenly gone. We stayed close to camp and did not sleep all night.

The next morning, we traveled along the Little Miami River to Clifton Mill. Robert heard it was the largest mill in the area and was known for having the least number of weevils in their flour. I was able to buy fresh eggs and pack them in corn meal. Mama said they would stay fresh for months.

Robert questioned the men at the mill about the native Indian we saw near our camp last night. They thought perhaps he is the one who watches over the travelers and helps them when they have troubles.

I sat on the porch of the mill, visiting with the local women. A kind lady told me how to make persimmon pudding. She thought the persimmons should be ripe enough to pick on our trail. She said the center of a persimmon can predict winter weather. When you slice it open, you will find one of three shapes in the center, a fork, a spoon, or a knife. If you find a fork, we will have a mild winter. A spoon means we will have lots of snow to shovel and a knife means you will have an extremely cold winter, with winds that will cut like a knife.

Feeling refreshed by our short visit at the mill, we are back on our trail. We watch closely for the native Indian in hopes we can communicate with him.

Every day brought the unexpected to the inexperienced travelers. Jane Ann's fear of the native Indians increased. Two or three watched them from the hillside most of the time. They often saw the one Indian near their camp.

Unknown to Robert or Jane Ann, their mule's hobble was cut and was taken during the night. The next morning, the one Indian brought the mules back. Without a word, he turned and disappeared into the woods. Perhaps, he was the one who keeps watch over the travelers. The men at the mill thought he had God in his heart, and that's why he helped the white settlers.

September 27, 1834

When I see our Indian friend, I raise my hand to wave and leave food for him on a stump or on a rock. I see him run to pick up the food, then he quickly disappears.

We saw what we thought was an abandoned wagon at the edge of the woods yesterday. We called, but no one answered. Nearby were six graves with matching crosses. Close by was a larger grave with a different kind of cross. Robert thought perhaps the family died of the fevers, and our Indian friend buried the last one that died.

Some things I wish we could forget, but they are forever etched in our memory. I think of the family who lays in silence and wondered if the same thing could happen to us. I pray for the families they may have left behind who might never know what happened to their loved ones. I am reminded of the words my father carved more with each day, "In God is our trust." I remember the sad, challenging days after he died when I would hear

Mama whisper those words when she was afraid. I am my mother's daughter, and I find myself whispering the same words as I again notice small groups of native Indians on the hillside.

Some wagons sit in silence along the trail where perhaps fevers or illness have wiped out entire families, often caused by contaminated water or food they shared or passed from one to the other.

Often, families back east never knew what happened to their loved ones. Sometimes the last survivor nailed a note to their wagon telling what happened to them. Others left names of family members for whoever found them to contact. Others wrote detailed journals, left unfinished.

September 29, 1834

A cool breeze is swirling the leaves of many colors along our trail. I am reminded of apple-picking time at the farm in Virginia. I miss our home, and I miss our family. I have battled my tears all day and refuse to let them start endlessly flowing.

As we bounced along in our wagon talking about how much we missed our brothers and the fun we had picking apples in the orchards, Robert suddenly stopped the wagon. He squeezed my hand and pointed to an opening in the trees. There stood over a dozen apple trees, covered with red apples. We laughed like kids as we jumped down from our wagon and ran to see our unexpected surprise. Robert climbed the tree to pick what we needed, leaving the rest for other families.

I smile as I finish writing for today. Only God knows our thoughts and could perfectly provide what our hearts

desire at just the right moment. I think of Mama teaching
me Psalms 18:30.

"As for God, Jane Ann, His way is perfect…"

"Oh, Grams," Lydia said, God is perfect! When Jane Ann and Robert were missing their family most, God surprised them with apples. They didn't need the apples, but he wanted them to know the blessing was from him. Not just a few apples but trees filled with them."

Putting her arm over Lydia's shoulder, Grams smiled and said, "You're pretty smart for a ten-year old little girl."

Lydia was tired and wanted to go to bed. Hugging Grams and Pops goodnight, she said, "I have a lot to thank God for, and you two are first on my list."

Thinking about how Jane Ann kneeled beside her bed to pray, Lydia fell to her knees. Laying her head on the side of her bed, she started thanking God, not asking for anything, just thanking him.

The next morning, after breakfast and a couple chores, they were anxious to return to reading Jane Ann's diary.

Pops wanted to read first.

September 30, 1834

Dark storm clouds covered us when we woke this morning.
In case the rains become heavy, Robert hooked the possum

belly on the bottom of the wagon to hold dry wood. I gathered wood as I walked beside our wagon. Soon, a torrential rain started to fall. I climbed on the wagon and covered Robert with a painted tarp. The rain was so heavy, the back wheels of the wagon stuck in the ruts of the front wheels.

Out of nowhere, we suddenly saw our Indian friend. Taking the reins of our mules, he led us out of the mud onto solid, grassy land. He motioned for us to angle our wagon toward a big rock overhang.

Climbing down from our wagon, we saw a cave that would give us shelter from the pouring rain. Robert hobbled the mules, and I tied down the cover on the wagon. We lit a torch, and we followed our friend into the cave to a small room-sized area.

We brought the dry wood in from the wagon to build a fire. I got food and blankets from the wagon.

We stayed inside the cave the rest of the day and made our beds to sleep for the night. The rain eventually stopped. We took food to our Indian friend and tried to communicate that he should stay in the cave with us. Instead, he stayed outside under the rock cliff as if he were there to protect us.

Robert was so tired, he fell sound asleep. I had never been in a cave, so I was too afraid to sleep. I lay still beside him. I started hearing sounds I had never heard before, so I woke him up.

Suddenly, the Indian rushed inside the cave, grabbed our blankets, covered us, and laid himself on top of the blankets. A loud swooshing sound horrified me. A colony of bats flew out from the deep darkness of the cave. When the sound stopped, he uncovered us and touched our arms to be sure we were not hurt.

*Robert grabbed his hand, and I grabbed his other hand,
trying to express our gratitude for saving our lives.*

The next morning our friend was gone.

*As we traveled the next day, I left apples and food to show
our appreciation. We sometimes saw him at a distance,
continuing to watch over us.*

The native Indian, who at first scared both Jane
Ann and Robert, slowly became their friend. The fear
they felt melted away as they saw him watch over
and care for them. He changed from being the quiet,
mysterious native Indian to a kindhearted friend.

Caves have always been used as a place of refuge
from weather and enemies. Many were hidden in
rock cliffs behind brush. The Native Indians in Ohio
used what is called the Olentangy Indian Caverns to
live in during winter and as a place of shelter during
storms. That might have been where Robert and Jane
Ann stayed during the rainstorm.

October 3, 1834

*We will soon return to the main road to Cincinnati where
we can travel much faster. If we had not taken the slow
side trails, we would never have met our friend. We are
forever thankful to him for saving our lives and helping
us when we did not know we were in danger. The night
our mules were taken, he must have followed the people
who stole them. Perhaps, he placed himself in danger to
get our mules back.*

*We have given him the name "Protector." When we stop,
he comes to sit with us and seems to enjoy our food. I*

used some of the apples to make a big cobbler. He liked it and wanted more the next day.

As I sit and write my thoughts, I want to think about what I am learning from Protector. The men at the mill might have been right. He must know God. He put himself in danger to help us, and I notice when we eat together, he takes his food last. I think it is the joy Mama taught us as children that I recognize in him.

I wonder what happened to his family and why he is alone. I asked Robert if we could take him on to Cincinnati, but he thinks Protector is called to be used by God right where he is for now.

Jane Ann continued to talk about the calling on Protector's life. He seemed never to hesitate in putting his life in danger to save others. Robert wondered how many times he placed himself between them and dangers they never knew existed.

October 5, 1834

At sunrise the next morning, I am in a panic for us to return to the road for Cincinnati. We knew last evening it would be our last night with Protector. He stays on the side trails to help people but not on the main road. As a small gift of our appreciation, Robert bent the handles off two silver spoons, laid them in the fire, hammered the edges smooth, and wired them together to make a cross.

As our farewell meal, I cooked apple cobbler and stew. We presented him with the silver spoon cross.

We could tell his heart was touched and in his own way, knew the special meaning of the cross. He pulled a small wooden box from his side pouch. Protector placed it in Robert's hand and closed his fingers around the box. Nodding his head to thank him, Robert opened his hand and turned the box over. We were shocked to see the side-cut apple carved on the top.

It was the box our father, Thomas Crawford, had given to Thomas L before leaving Virginia. We tried to ask Protector where he obtained the box and what happened to Thomas L, but he could not understand. He kept touching his heart and showed us a wound on his thumb. We had no idea what he was trying to tell us. Our parents, Thomas L, and little Charles left right after the wedding to go on to Cincinnati to visit Uncle Charles. They were more than a week ahead of us in travel.

I kept asking myself over and over again, "What could have happened to Thomas L for him to give Protector his treasured apple seed box?" Neither of us thinks Protector would steal the box or harm Thomas L.

The travelers had no communication or way to find out where their family was or what happened to Thomas L. All they could do is once again place their hope and trust in God and press forward to Cincinnati as fast as possible.

"What do you think could have happened, Pops?" Lydia asked, concerned.

"I don't know. I hope nothing bad happened to Thomas L or the rest of the family." Pops shook his head, turned the page, and kept reading.

October 7, 1834

Neither of us slept all night. Instead, we prayed. Still in darkness, I held the lantern for Robert as he prepared the wagon for travel. We pulled out as the sun was rising. Frightening thoughts rolled over and over in my mind about what may have happened to Thomas L. We stopped at the first supply store on the main road, but no one remembered seeing the Catts/Crawford wagon. The rest of the day, we gave a yell at everyone we passed, but no one had seen them. One traveler called out to tell us we were about twenty miles from Cincinnati.

To stop the carousel of thoughts, I searched my heart for a Scripture I could use to call out to God.

"Fear thou not, Jane Ann, for I am with thee" (Isaiah 41:10).

I closed my eyes and prayed.

Each mile seemed to take forever. Anxious thoughts filled my mind. My heart pounded as the worn wagon wheels creeped along. Robert held my hand tightly and said, "In God is our trust, Jane Ann." As in the past, the words brought comfort to my heart.

Since the main road was easier to travel, we kept going even into the evening. I held the lantern high so Robert could see the road as we traveled onward to Cincinnati.

"It's hard to imagine not being able to communicate with my family," Lydia suddenly said. "My brother and sister want to know everything I've been doing while I'm at the farm."

"Do you remember Alexander Graham Bell had the same challenge you and I have—dyslexia?" Grams asked. "Even though he invented the telephone and received a U.S. patent in 1876, the telephone was not commonly used until 1900 to 1910. Then the transcontinental telephone line started operating in 1915."

"It took that long for communications to develop. Yet you, Lydia, have grown up with instant communication at your fingertips. But keep in mind in the past how God helped people communicate through their hearts, and he still does. If you can't stop thinking about someone, it could be God letting you know you need to check on them."

Lydia nodded. "That's why I called Mom last night before going to sleep. I thought about her all day yesterday. She didn't tell me why, only that she had a bad day and was glad I called. It would be so hard to think someone you love might be in danger, and you can't call them, like Jane Ann's situation with Thomas L," she added.

October 9, 1834

The last stretch of road took longer than we expected. In the dark of night, we pulled our wagon in front of Uncle Charles's home in Cincinnati, weary and achy all over. With no lights shinning in the windows, we were uncertain if we should knock on the door. Even though exhausted, a deep concern for Thomas L came over me, and I could not contain myself. I jumped from our wagon, rushed to the door, and began knocking while Robert tied our horse and mules to the hitching post.

Uncle Charles opened the door slightly and with his pistol in hand, demanded to know who I was. Robert ran up on the porch and responded, "It is Robert and Jane Ann Crawford. We are looking for Thomas L Catts."

In a gruff-grumpy voice, he responded, "He is sleeping, you silly boy!"

The heavy shackles of worry fell from me at that moment. I was so relieved to know he was alive and sleeping. Again, one moment changed my life.

Since the entire house was now awake, Uncles Charles insisted Robert and Jane Ann come inside. Barely through the door, Jane Ann looked up and saw her brother Thomas L coming down the stairs in his long, white nightshirt, yawning. She rushed to the bottom of the stairs and threw her arms around him.

The confused look on his face showed he had no idea what was going on.

Uncle Charles questioned the reason for this abrupt visit in the middle of the night.

As his response, Robert pulled the apple seed box from his pocket and laid it in Thomas L's hand.

"Why do you have this box?" Thomas L asked, still half asleep. "Did you meet my blood brother on the trail? Oh no, did something happen to him?"

Neither Robert nor Jane Ann responded.

Hearing someone coming down the stairs, Jane Ann glanced up to see her Mama carrying little Charles, with Papa a step behind them. She ran to meet them and tried to explain why they thought something had happened to Thomas L.

Grumpy Uncle Charles suggested they discuss the story in the morning and let him get some sleep.

October 10, 1834

Since we realized how unexpected our middle of the night arrival was, we slept in our wagon until morning. As exhausted as we were, we knew we had questions that needed to be answered. We were so thankful to see Thomas L was safe; however, we still wanted him to answer our questions.

This morning when we softly knocked on the door, Uncle Charles greeted us with a smile and a warm welcome. As we walked into the dining room where breakfast was to be served, Robert quietly whispered in my ear that we must never again wake Uncle Charles in the middle of the night.

After breakfast Uncle Charles suggested we gather in the parlor to discuss our concerns. Immediately, Robert apologized for our rudeness in waking up the entire house in the middle of the night. He explained to his Uncle Charles how much I loved my brother and how I could not rest until I was sure he was safe.

After telling them the story about our friend, Protector, I ended by saying, "We were so afraid something horrible had happened to Thomas L."

Thomas L, sitting next to me, reached over, put his arm around my shoulder, and told me how much he loved and appreciated me. He told me I had been his protector after our Papa died.

My emotions and exhaustion welled up in my heart, and I began to cry.

We still had questions to ask Thomas L, but Uncle Charles, a wise man beyond measure, suggested he be allowed to tell his side of the story. Everyone agreed.

THOMAS L TELLS HIS STORY

After the wedding, we left for Cincinnati. We too were told the main road had been washed away and were advised to take the side trail. Not long after we started the trail, a lone Indian started watching and following us.

After a long day traveling, we found a place to camp for the night. Papa had untied his horse from the back of the wagon and was starting to unharness the mules. Mama was stacking rocks in a circle for our fire while I gathered wood. Little Charles was asleep in the wagon.

"Out of nowhere, a bobcat leapt from a tall tree toward the mules. In fear, they reared up and started running. Papa and I rushed after the wagon. He tripped over a rock and fell to his knees while I kept running as fast as I could. The jarring motion woke Charles, and I could see him standing in the back of the wagon crying.

Suddenly, the native Indian we saw earlier rode up beside the mules, grabbed the reins, and stopped the runaway wagon. He calmed the mules while he waited for me to reach the wagon. Looking into my eyes, he handed me the reins. Without a word, he rode away.

I settled the mules, tied them to a tree, and hurried to lift little Charles from the wagon. Untying the mules, I climbed into the wagon with Charles securely in my arms and returned to where we were making camp.

Thankful Charles was not harmed; Papa and Mama thought we should find a way to thank our Indian friend.

We continued to see him watch over us. One afternoon while Mama and little Charles were picking berries, he walked over close to them. He reached out his hand to Mama and took the berries from her hand. Throwing them toward the woods he shook his head as if to say no. Then he was suddenly gone. Frightened, Mama grabbed Charles and ran back to camp. She told Papa what happened and described the berries she was picking. Papa looked upward as if to thank God and explained the berries were poisonous pokeberries.

The following day, we were packing our wagon after breakfast. Mama noticed little Charles was gone. We franticly searched the area but could not find him. I saddled Papa's horse to look for Charles. I rode across a narrow meadow toward a high hill. Glancing up, I could see my little brother standing on a rock ledge, looking down. I rode as fast as I could while still keeping him in sight.

Suddenly, my horse stumbled, fell, and threw me to the ground. I jumped up and started running. I looked up just as our Indian friend slowly walked up to Charles, knelt down beside him as if talking to him, and picked him up. As I ran closer, he walked downhill toward me with Charles in his arms.

Winded, I fell to the ground, just as our friend handed Charles to me. Making sure he was alright, I thanked God.

The Indian's horse was tied to a nearby tree. He helped little Charles and me onto his horse, and he led us back to camp. We tried to thank him, but he instead turned to ride away. Within moments, he stopped, turned the horse around, dismounted, and handed me the rope tied around his horse's neck. I realized he was giving me his horse. He silently walked away. He must have known Papa's horse was severely injured from the fall. We later found Papa's saddle near our wagon.

The next morning, Papa thought we should find our friend and again try to thank him. We searched until we found him in the nearby meadow. Little Charles ran to him and grabbed his hand. He tugged on his hand until he understood Charles wanted him to go with us.

He walked back to our camp, sat with us for a long while and ate supper with us. We tried to communicate with him but were uncertain if he understood. He continued to follow us on foot each day and would eat with us in the evenings.

Our last night before getting back on the main road, he again ate with us. He must have known it was our last night together. Smiling, he presented me with a leather pouch.

Wanting to return his kindness with a meaningful gift, I remembered showing him Papa's apple seed box and how to plant the apple seeds. I looked at Papa for approval, and he nodded. I pulled the apple seed box from my pocket and laid it in our friend's hand.

Again, he smiled. Pulling his knife from his side pouch, he made a cut on his thumb. He handed me the knife. Somehow, I understood. I cut my thumb and we pressed our blood together. He pointed at me and touched his heart. I did the same. I leaned over and hugged my blood brother.

Even though the apple seed box was a family treasure, Papa thought it was a small gift to give to someone who had saved Charles's life three times and had given us his horse.

Everyone sat quietly amazed by two totally different stories about their same Indian friend.

Jane Ann picked up the apple seed box and laid it in Thomas L's hand. With a smile, she said to him, "It is a gift from your blood brother, our friend, Protector."

Henry David Thoreau was quoted, "Our truest life is when we are in dreams awake."

At this time in America, people feared Indians and did not make friends with them easily. The hearts of the Catts/Crawford family tore down the wall of fear and opened their hearts to Protector. He showed them what they feared could instead be loved.

After Jane Ann gave the apple seed box back to Thomas L, he held up his thumb and tapped on his chest and reminded everyone of the Scripture in Matthew. "With men this is impossible; but with God all things are possible."

October 11, 1834

I am so deeply thankful for my family. When I think about what might have happened to my brother Charles, I am forever grateful to God. And we will never forget our friend, Protector. Tomorrow my family will leave Robert and me behind for him to read law with Uncle Charles. Mama made Papa promise they would not leave for Missouri until we arrived safely, and she could tell us goodbye. Uncertain when we will see each other again, I know it will be a heart-breaking moment for us all.

I pray Mama will have a happy life in Missouri.

For as long as I can remember, I have asked God to make me strong and wise like Mama and to teach me to be compassionate to others. As my heart breaks when we say goodbye, I will follow her example. I will stand strong at my husband's side and face our future together.

JOHN'S BEEFY STEW

3 Tablespoons olive oil
4 Tablespoons butter
3 ½ pound of lean stew meat
1 large sweet onion chopped
1 Tablespoon minced garlic
3 Tablespoons Worcestershire sauce
7 cups beef broth, more if needed
3 Tablespoons sugar
1 small can tomato paste
2 teaspoons salt and 2 teaspoons pepper
1 ½ teaspoons paprika
Cook until tender in salt water:
7 carrots, cut into thick circles
3 celery ribs chopped
3 pounds of peeled potatoes
Add:
2 cans diced tomatoes
1 ½ Tablespoons flour

Heat oil and butter together in a large pan. Add beef and brown on all sides. Remove beef from pan and set aside. Cook garlic and onions until soft. Add beef broth, Worcestershire sauce, tomato paste, sugar, paprika, salt and pepper. Put meat back in pan.

Cover and simmer on low for 2 hours or longer if needed to get beef tender. Add more broth if needed.

If meat is tender, drain carrots, celery, and potatoes. Add to stew along with tomatoes.

If broth of stew is thin, remove 1 cup of broth,

mix in 1 ½ Tablespoons of flour. Slowly add back into stew until it is as thick as you like.

Cover and simmer for 10 minutes before serving.

Best when served with cornbread sticks or angel biscuits and Winesap apple pie.

CHAPTER 6

Yet another day came when Jane Ann and her family had to painfully say goodbye. She knew her family felt it was God's call to go west. With that understanding, she asked God to give her the strength and courage she would need.

October 12, 1834

Robert and I stood together waving goodbye to our family until we could no longer see them. This painful moment I will never forget. My kindhearted husband squeezed my hand and took me for a walk in the garden behind Uncle Charles's home. We sat on a swing in the garden where Robert held me close and listened to me cry.

With pain-filled hearts, the Catts/Crawford family said goodbye to their son, daughter, sister, and brother. They took a deep breath of courage, filled their hearts with hope, and answered God's call to go west. They firmly placed their feet on the words "In God is our trust" as they again left part of their family behind.

In a whisper, Lydia said, "I know how it feels to tell your family goodbye. I wanted more than anything to stay with you and Pops." With her lip quivering, Lydia said, "But I still miss my family."

Sitting next to Lydia, Pops pulled her close for a hug. "You'll see them soon, and until then, we have a puzzle to solve about Jane Ann and Robert. How about you read from the diary for a while?"

"Okay," she said, taking the diary from Pops. She was happy to see the next page was about Christmas, her favorite holiday.

Christmas 1834

A traveling preacher brought us a letter today from Mama. I am so relieved to hear they safely crossed the Mississippi River and are settled for winter at Saint Genevieve, Missouri. She wrote about the challenges they faced on their travels and warned me about the dangers of crossing the river. In her compassionate words, she described the day a ferry turned over in the river. I could sense her sadness for the two little orphaned boys who were left behind. Mama wrote that she cared for them until she found them a good home.

I continue to ask God to give me a compassionate heart like Mama's, which flows so naturally when someone needs love.

Robert and I appreciate Uncle Charles. He spends many hours teaching Robert about the importance of law and order as our county grows. He thinks Robert will be a fine young lawyer and enjoys allowing him to attend court cases with him so he can experience both sides of the court process.

I keep busy working on my reading and sewing. I have again found my resting place on the swing in the garden behind the house. On cold days, I wrap warmly and sit with the crisp winter breeze to my back while I read my Bible. I enjoy finding Scriptures to memorize as God's promises to me and for those I love.

This will be our first Christmas without our family. Uncle Charles has been especially kind to make Robert and me feel welcome in his home. But we feel emptiness away from family. We go to our knees each night and pray for God to protect and guide our family in both Missouri and Virginia.

Robert felt privileged and honored to read law with his uncle, the Honorable Judge Charles Hammond. He learned the importance of state's right from him. Uncle Charles wanted Robert to learn early in his career that each state should have the right to make laws which will best serve the people of their state.

In years past, President John Adams asked Judge Hammond to serve on the United States Supreme Court. He graciously declined due to opposing political views.

Christmas had always been a joyful family time for Robert and Jane Ann. However, to be a guest in someone's home during the holidays made them hesitant to follow their family traditions.

To surprise Robert, Jane Ann brought a knife and an apple up to their room. He was happy to cut the apple, tell her the story of the Bethlehem Star, and read the Christmas story to his beloved wife. She thought perhaps he was practicing for when they had a family of their own.

Spring 1835

After years of hard work and practice, my reading has improved, and my eyes are better at separating the words. I sat in the swing reading Pilgrim's Progress while I watched a kaleidoscope of butterflies hover above the colorful milkweed flowers. I was especially amused by the tiny birds which sip the nectar from the flowers. Wise Uncle Charles let me know they are called hummingbirds. No matter where I am, spring is my most favorite time of year.

I often wonder what has happened to our friend, Protector. I pray for his safety while he helps others. Robert has promised before we leave Ohio, we will go back to the side trail to find him. Uncle Charles thinks we are foolish, but we still plan to go.

I sometimes feel lost while Robert reads law with Uncle Charles. I wish I could find a job, but the society ladies would frown upon me working, and they would look unfavorably at Robert. So, I decided to do what Mama did in the past. I talked to several neighbor ladies about my hats, and they would like to see my designs. Perhaps I can make hats as a way to save money for when we start our family and make our move to Missouri. Once again, the tarnished silver thimble Mama gave me will be of good use.

A letter arrived from a friend of Robert's father, named John Marshall Clemens. Like Thomas

Crawford, he was a lawyer from Virginia. He and
his wife, Jane, would be traveling through Cincinnati
on their move to Missouri. He offered to take a letter
or whatever was needed to Robert's parents as they
passed through Saint Geneviève. And he had a letter
for Jane Ann from her brother George.

Jane Ann got busy crocheting a shawl for her
mama and made some taffy candy to send to Thomas
L and Charles. Robert gathered several law books to
send with Mr. Clemens, which he thought his father
might need.

When Mr. and Mrs. Clemens arrived in
Cincinnati, Jane Ann and Robert met them in the
parlor. As Uncle Charles walked in the parlor, he
noticed Mrs. Clemens was expecting a baby. He
offered for them to stay the night, and they accepted.

The next morning after breakfast, Jane Ann
packed leftover baked custard and butter-horn rolls
for the Clemens. They were soon on the pioneer
trail to Missouri where they would see Thomas and
Frances Crawford.

Jane Ann quietly slipped away to the swing in the
garden to read the letter from her beloved brother,
George.

My dearest sister Jane Ann,

*Words are not adequate to tell you how much I miss you.
I sometimes think I should leave Virginia behind and go
to Missouri as I promised Mama. We could have a long
visit on my way, and perhaps I could help you and Robert
prepare for your move to Missouri as well.*

For now, I have a good reason to stay in Virginia. I have met a beautiful young lady with long dark hair and big blue eyes that seems to melt my heart. Her name is Mary Ann Tarr. She is part of the naval commander, Commodore Matthew Perry's family. She walks past the mercantile most every day, glancing in the window, hoping I will notice her. I look forward to seeing her and will ask permission to court her soon. It seems her father is not pleased I am not seeking a military career. If God has chosen her to be my wife, even her father cannot stop our love for one another. I have told her all about you, my little sister.

I am busy working for Mr. Patterson at the Wellsburg Mercantile. His wife, Ms. Ileane, hopes he will one day sell the mercantile to me. She introduced me to Mary Ann and hopes we will get married.

The apple trees are so beautiful and have an abundance of blossoms which our Crawford brothers are happy to see. Unless we have a late frost, there will be a bumper crop of apples in the fall. They send their love and regards to you and Robert.

Oh, how I miss our family. I am thankful Mama has Papa and they are happy in Missouri. With every letter, she reminds me of my promise. I will one day, but for now the lady of my dreams keeps me here.

Please tell my blood brother, Robert, I miss him. I know he will be a fine lawyer one day. My heart will always be with you, Jane Ann. And my prayers are constantly with you.

Your loving brother,

George

Fall 1835

With some of the money Uncle Charles pays Robert to work in his office, I purchased beautiful fabric for hats. I have sold seven hats and have orders for twelve more. I wrote to Mama to tell her I am using Grandmother Neal's silver thimble to sew hats. I think she will be most pleased.

Uncle Charles greatly dislikes the idea of me selling hats. However, he feels he must compliment the ladies at church who parade past him wearing my hats. I chuckle at his compliments which I think he wants me to hear.

Robert will soon have a few days off from work while Uncle Charles goes to Cleveland for court. As he promised, we will go back to the side trails to see if we can find Protector. I made him a coat and a crazy quilt to keep him warm. Not knowing how to sew leather, I traded a hat with Mr. Williams, the supply store owner, for a pair of warm moccasins. His wife, Ms. Joan, will be most pleased when he brings home the hat she has had her eye on for months. Robert wants to take dried apple rings and dried beef to Protector so he has food for winter. I will take an apple cobbler and keep praying we can find our friend.

Before leaving, we received a letter from Mama and Papa. They had a long visit with Mr. and Mrs. Clemens and thanked us for the items we sent. She wrote about later receiving a letter from the Clemenses, letting them know they were settled in a village called Florida, Missouri.

Jane Ann and Robert left early one morning in their quest to find Protector. They first inquired at the supply store before they turned toward the side trail. No one had heard about him in a long time.

As they traveled the trail, they asked everyone they met if they had seen a native Indian watching them or who had helped them. They all shook their heads and kept going. Robert and Jane Ann worried that something might have happened to him.

Three days later

I am forever grateful. We finally found Protector in an open field near the cave we camped in on our trip to Cincinnati. We waved to him, and he ran fast to see us. Robert and he hugged like long lost brothers. He approached me, gently hugged me, and then tapped on his chest as he looked at each of us. Taking me by my hand, he pulled me toward the cave.

Still remembering the fear I felt when the bats swarmed from deep inside the cave, I was reluctant to go. Robert took my other hand to comfort me. As we approached the cave, Protector called out what seemed to be a name. From inside the cave, a woman stepped out with a tiny baby in her arms.

We were overjoyed to see Protector had a family. His wife stepped forward and laid their baby boy in my arms. Protector lifted his thumb and rubbed it. He then tapped on his chest and tapped on his baby boy's chest and said, "Thomas." Tears filled my eyes as I thought about how pleased my brother would be to know that his blood brother had named his son after him.

The next morning before we left to go back to Cincinnati, we shared breakfast together. I brought an apple cobbler for Protector, and he shared his fish with us. We then gave them the moccasins, quilt, coat, and the food.

Protector pulled on Robert's hand to go with him. Out in the open meadow, he showed him tiny apple trees he had planted from the seeds Thomas L gave him. Robert thought this was perhaps how he honored Thomas L.

We prepared to leave. After communicating our goodbyes, Robert and I climbed on our wagon, and our horses pulled us forward. Looking back, Protector had the coat and moccasins on, and his wife had the quilt wrapped around her. I suddenly asked Robert to stop the wagon. I jumped down and took the shawl I was wearing and wrapped it around their baby. Protector's wife hugged me tightly and tapped her heart. I tearfully walked away and did not look back. I knew our paths would never cross again.

As we pulled away, Robert snuggled me close, wrapped his coat around me, kissed my cheek, and whispered into my ear, "God answered your prayer. You have Mama's compassionate heart."

I am forever grateful God answered my prayer. Protector has a family to love him just as he has loved others.

"A new commandment I give unto you, Jane Ann, that ye love one another; as I have loved you." (John 13:34).

Robert and Jane would never forget the lessons they learned from their Indian friend. They understood how to love unconditionally all that God created. Red and yellow, black and white—we're all precious in God's sight and should be in ours as well.

A few weeks before Christmas, Robert and Jane Ann received a thank you letter from Mr. and Mrs. Clemens. They said they were settled in Missouri, and he had opened a mercantile. They wanted them to know their son was born on November 30, 1835.

They named him Samuel Clemens, and they would soon be moving to the nearby town of Hannibal, Missouri.

Spring 1836

Spring flowers are in bloom, and women in Cincinnati are looking for new Easter hats. Since I do not have a shop, the ladies stop by Uncle Charles house asking if they can speak to the hat maker. He does not find humor in the idea of me earning extra money making hats or that his house keeper is inconvenienced.

Mama taught me to solve one problem at a time. I have inquired at Mrs. Gibson's dress shop to see if she will sell my hats for me. This and a new top hat I will make for Uncles Charles should solve my problem.

Robert and Jane Ann made the decision to move to Missouri the following spring. The newsy letters from her mother about life in Missouri aroused their interest in homesteading land. Their father offered for Robert to work in his Springfield law practice. More families are moving to southwest Missouri, and Thomas thinks another lawyer will be needed.

Each hat Jane Ann sold added to the money they were saving for their move. The hardest part they thought would be telling Uncle Charles. To their surprise, he encouraged them to follow their dream to go west while they were still young.

October 17, 1836

Robert is coming home early to take me to Mr. Mecklenburg's house for German food. He sets tables in his side garden once a year for people to experience German food and music. He is teaching his sons how cooking is done in the old country and hopes to open a restaurant one day.

My dear husband is excited to celebrate my birthday. However, I have a surprise for him. I am expecting a baby in the spring. Robert will love his surprise for the rest of his life.

Jane Ann had waited patiently for God to bless them with a baby. She and Robert laughed as they talked about where the baby will be born—Ohio or Missouri.

Later, while sitting on the porch swing, Robert heard one of the neighbors playing the most popular song of the year on his fiddle, "Turkey In The Straw."

Spring 1837

It is hard to believe we are preparing for our move to Missouri. Our baby is due sometime in May. Robert thinks if we leave by April 1, I will be with Mama in time for the baby to be born. Mama and Papa have added a room onto their cabin for us to live in until we can find a place of our own. Since this is our first child, I am comforted to think Mama will be with me to help with the delivery.

I am sewing all my fabrics to make hats so we will have money for our travels. Mrs. Gibson is telling her customers I am moving. They all want to purchase a hat. She thinks she will soon be sold out.

Uncle Charles has been kind to us for two years. He is proud of Robert and sees him as the son he never had.

At his age, he knows he will never be able to travel to Missouri to see us, and we know we may never pass this way again. We can't help but feel the sadness of knowing once we leave, we will never see him again.

The week before Jane Ann and Robert were to leave, Uncle Charles planned a surprise for them. Months before, he had written to their brother George, extending and invitation for him to visit before their move. George traveled two-hundred and fifty miles on horseback to see his sister and brother.

As Jane Ann and Robert sat down for dinner with Uncle Charles, they noticed an extra place-setting on the table. While questioning if they were having a dinner guest, Jane Ann heard a knock at the door. Uncle Charles asked her if she would see who it was.

Before opening the stained-glass door, she could see the silhouette of a tall man. Opening the door, she was surprised to see her brother George. She excitedly hugged him tightly and said, "You are who the extra plate is for."

They walked arm-in-arm to the dining room.

Uncle Charles looked at Jane Ann and asked, "Do you like your surprise?"

Laughter and chatter sounded throughout Uncle Charles's house. Later in the evening, George mentioned to Robert that he met a beautiful young lady named Mary Ann. If all goes as expected with their courting, he hopes to marry her, and one day bring her to Missouri.

A week of making memories and sharing stories quickly passed. The moment arrived for them to say their goodbyes to Uncle Charles and George. Hugging each of them, Jane Ann expressed how much she loved them. With a determined heart of courage, Jane Ann and Robert climbed onto their wagon and rolled westward.

Crying as they pulled away, Jane Ann asked Robert to stop. She climbed down from their wagon and ran back to hug George and Uncle Charles one last time. She knew she would never see Uncle Charles again but had no idea it would be fifteen years before she would see her brother George.

CHAPTER 7

April 15, 1837

Our travels have been successful thus far across Ohio and Indiana. I have trouble sleeping at night in our wagon and seem to be extra tired. Robert insists I lay in the back of the wagon part of the day to rest. He wants me and the baby healthy and strong. However, I want to sit with Robert as much as possible so I can enjoy the beautiful places I have never seen.

A family we visited with one afternoon suggested we stop at Boone's Mill while in Indiana if we needed supplies. A short distance off the road, Robert thought it best for us to spend the night near the mill so we had fresh water for our animals.

The mill was built by the famous pioneer Daniel Boone's brother, Squire Boone. He was an explorer, statesman, minister, and a Patriot soldier in the Revolutionary War. A lady at the mill said he had been wounded in eleven battles and showed us the inscription he carved on the foundation stone of the mill.

"My God my life hath much befriended. I will praise him till my days are ended." She said he never stopped thanking God for saving him during his many battles.

As I sat on a big rock with my feet in the cool water near the mill, I could see Scriptures Mr. Boone had carved on the outside walls of a cavern.

For a young couple following their dream and desiring to see family, the journey was difficult but exciting. They faced rain and hailstorms, loud, flashing, lightning storms which were scary and dangerous, and snakes that spooked the mules, causing them to rare up and run wild. Getting them under control took strong arms and skill.

Every sunrise brought new challenges and every sunset brought tired bodies thankful to have survived another day on the pioneer trail west.

The need for help or shelter often happened at inopportune times. The day-to-day rough wagon ride through Illinois was perhaps what caused Jane Ann to go into labor early. She woke up not feeling well, so Robert insisted she lay in the wagon to rest. Hearing her groaning in pain, he knew Jane Ann must be having birthing pains. He began searching for another wagon on the trail or a farmhouse where they could find help. He saw a house to the south, so he yanked the mule reins that direction. Pulling his wagon near the barn, he yelled for help. A young couple came running out and suggested Robert carry Jane Ann into the house.

The lady, Mrs. Blevins, could tell the baby was about to be born. Mr. Blevins and their son, Mason, tried to calm Robert while they waited.

The heartwarming sound of a healthy cry soon echoed from the bedroom. Jane Ann had a baby girl. Their baby would be named Helen Frances Crawford. Helen was Robert's mother's name and Frances was

Jane Ann and later, Robert's mother's name. The baby was small, so they stayed several days.

Soon, Jane Ann felt strong enough to continue their journey. Mr. Blevins and Mason made sure Robert and Jane Ann had plenty of food and their water barrels full. Before leaving, Mrs. Blevins gave Robert a crock of fresh cream. She showed him where to set it under the wagon seat. The bouncing motion of the wagon would turn the cream into butter by evening. Since baby Helen Frances was small, butter would help her gain weight. Their act of kindness was never to be forgotten.

God, who brought the love of Robert and Jane Ann together, had now sealed it with a child.

Late April 1837

Baby Helen Frances is growing, and I am gaining strength. We will soon cross over the Mississippi River. I will not tell Robert the closer we get, the more frightened I become. I cannot stop thinking about the family who drowned, leaving behind two young boys. I hold my sweet baby close. I remember the Scripture and fill in my name just I did when I was a little girl.

"What time I, Jane Ann, am afraid, I will trust in Thee" (Psalms 56:3).

God's ways are perfect. As planned, Robert and Jane Ann used most of their food, emptied their water barrels, and were prepared to cross the mighty Mississippi River. When Robert pulled their wagon to the ferry lane, no other families were waiting to cross. The sun shined brightly with not a cloud in the blue sky. Robert unhitched the mules and loaded them and the horse on one ferry. He paid a young man to ride over with the livestock so he could ride with Jane Ann, the baby, and their wagon on a separate ferry. Sensitive to her fears, Robert stayed at her side as they crossed the river.

May 1, 1837

We praised God that we safely crossed the river. Tired and needing supplies, we stayed two nights in the French settlement town of Saint Genevieve, Missouri. This is where Mama and Papa stayed during the winter of 1834.

Robert inquired in town about Mrs. Sammons who Mama said took the two little boys, Willie and Pete. We knocked on her door and explained who we were. She welcomed us in, prepared a hot meal, and insisted we stay in her home.

Oh, how wonderful it felt to sleep in a bed and eat food that was not cooked on a campfire spit. She made us feel like family and asked that we deliver a letter to our parents on her behalf.

"That must be the letter we found in the wooden box," Lydia interrupted. "It was a thank you note from Mrs. Sammons."

"Yes," Grams said. "Did you understand how God supplied for their needs? Frances Catts/Crawford took care of Willie and Pete, and Mrs. Sammons took care of Jane Ann and her family," Grams explained.

"God wants his circle of life to continue, so we help one another."

In a letter Jane Ann received before leaving Cincinnati, Frances mentioned a freshwater spring near the Meramec River that would be a good resting place after leaving Saint Genevieve.

The name Meramec means "ugly fish." Local Indians thought the catfish in the stream looked ugly.

After long days of travel, they approached the spring, where they saw men on horses and in wagons. Robert walked toward them to inquire if he and Jane Ann would be able to stay a few nights along the stream to clean their wagon and wash clothes. The gentleman in charge was named Captain William Clark, Missouri's first Territorial Governor.

He was there overseeing the clearing of trails across Missouri for the American Indians coming from the Carolina states due to the Indian Removal Act.

Robert introduced himself and said he was from Virginia. Captain Clark, also from Virginia, now lived in Saint Louis. Captain Clark invited Robert and Jane Ann with their new baby to have supper with him at his camp that night. He told them about his journey west in 1804, at the request of President Jefferson, on what became known as the Lewis and Clark Expedition. The need for mapping and documenting the journey was of utmost importance for America to expand west.

Mesmerized by his stories and knowing the important part of history Captain Clark played, Robert was honored to have supper with him. He realized what an amazing, chance meeting they had encountered with Captain Clark. A story they would tell their children and grandchildren.

Captain Clark passed away the following year in Saint Louis with his family at his side.

$\longrightarrow$

"I've studied the Lewis and Clark Expedition," Lydia said, "and have been to the Museum in Saint Louis."

"Their journey expanded America," Pops told her. "And they were the first explorers to go all the way to the Pacific Ocean. Captain Lewis took his dog, Seaman, with him on the journey. While roaming the wild woods, Seaman encountered a grizzly bear. Captain Lewis killed the bear, used it for food and was the first to record seeing one of the giant bears.

"They never saw a grizzly bear before then?"

Grams smiled at Lydia. "Remember, they had no communication back then, and no one from the United States had ever been that far west."

"I just can't imagine what a different place this was back then," Lydia said.

"Lunch time is soon I hope." Pops said, as he walked over to look across the rain soaked green fields of the farm. "Yes life was different then. It's hard to imagine Kickapoo and Osage Indians once lived on this farm. And what it must have looked like when the Catts/Crawford family first arrived. It's difficult to think how hard it was just to survive during those early years. Lydia, maybe one day you'll write a diary that someone will find more than a hundred years later and read about your life."

After lunch Lydia was the first one back to the porch. She was excited to continue reading the story about someone who walked the fields of the farm and perhaps sat on the porch in the evenings, watching the pond. Jane Ann's life story had come alive to Lydia, and she couldn't wait to get started reading again.

May 10, 1837

We are nearing Springfield where we will see Mama and Papa. There is no way of telling them we are on our way and will arrive day after tomorrow. My heart pounds with excitement to see their faces. Three years is a long time we have waited to see them.

On May 12, 1837, Robert, Jane Ann, and baby Helen Frances arrived in Springfield, Missouri. They stopped at the first mercantile in town, and Robert hopped down from the wagon to go inside to ask where they might find the home of Thomas and Frances Crawford.

Jane Ann waited in the wagon with baby Helen Frances asleep in her arms. She heard Robert's voice coming from behind the wagon and another familiar voice. She glanced over to see who he was talking with. When she saw her brother Thomas L, she beamed with excitement. He climbed up to sit beside her and gave Robert directions to their cabin. Jane Ann leaned her head over onto Thomas L's shoulder and told him how much she had missed him. She could hardly wait to see her Mama and Papa.

When they drove up to the cabin, the door opened, and Frances stepped out. Jane Ann looked into the eyes of her Mama who she hadn't seen for three years. Frances ran to greet her daughter as Thomas L helped her and the baby down from the wagon.

Leaning toward her Mama, Jane Ann said, "Meet you first granddaughter, Helen Frances."

Smiling, tears filled Frances eyes as Jane Ann laid the tiny baby into her arms.

Thomas L ran to his Papa's office to tell him Mama needed him to hurry home as soon as possible.

When he arrived, he was surprised and overjoyed to see his son, Robert, and Jane Ann and to hold their baby, named after his first wife and Frances.

Jane Ann and Robert were finally back with their family once again.

News quickly passed through town that they had arrived.

One moment changes life. A new generation is added to a family.

Summer 1837

We are so thankful to be with family. I am learning how to live in a cabin in a small town. Life is much different here than at Uncle Charles's big house in the big city of Cincinnati or in the big city of Baltimore where I grew up. I am amazed how Mama has adapted to pioneer life. Friends are like family.

Robert enjoys working with Papa. He shares what he learned while reading law with Uncle Charles and his time in court. The Campbell and Fulbright families, both founding families of Springfield, welcome him as a new attorney.

One morning while Helen Frances took her nap, Mama worked inside. I stepped out to the garden to pick vegetables for canning.

Charles tagged along with me to check his watermelon patch. He wanted to educate me on growing watermelons. Gently looking at the bottom side of his largest melon, he said, "If it is yellow, it is ready to pull from the vine."

I did not tell Charles, but Mama poured sugar around the roots of his melons so they would be extra sweet melons for our Fourth of July picnic.

I am proud of myself. This city girl is learning to be a pioneer woman quiet well. I give God the credit, but I have to be willing to work with him.

No matter who you are or where you live in the United States of America, the Fourth of July Independence Day celebration is important. Time stops for all to remember those who gave their life, as did many men in the Catts/Crawford family, to keep America a free nation. Frances and Thomas respectfully and carefully showed their friends the piece of the Star-Spangled Banner Flag. The wooden sign they displayed on their porch on July Fourth. The words, "In God Is Our Trust," became the motto for other families as well.

JUST A MOMENT

After seeing the women wearing bonnets at the celebration, Jane Ann realized Springfield was not yet a fancy hat town. She made baby Helen Frances, her Mama, and herself each a new bonnet.

Christmas 1837

I have been helping Mama prepare our family Christmas dinner. I walked over to the tiny window of our cabin to look outside at the falling snow. My mind drifted back to the cold winter days in which I looked out our big window down at the snowy streets of Baltimore. Deep in my memories, I could faintly hear the Christmas bells ringing at the Old Otterbein Church. Thoughts of our last Christmas with Papa raced through my mind. I can almost feel the crisp, cold winter breeze on my face as we rode with the Crawford boys in the horse-drawn red sleigh.

My thoughts are suddenly broken by the sound of Helen Frances laughing at Papa bouncing her on his knee. Robert is playing marbles with Charles in front of the hearth. Thomas L is tuning up his fiddle to play Christmas carols. Mama is humming songs while she finishes the Sweet-Milk Cookies for Christmas morning. I smell the hickory fire roasting the Christmas turkey, apple pies in the oven, and I see one apple sitting on the mantel waiting for Papa to slice as he tells the story of the Bethlehem Star. I glanced around the room and realized how blessed we are to be together. But oh, how I wish George could be with us.

December in Springfield was extremely cold that year, with over a foot of snow covering the ground.

According to Mr. Dike's aching bones, more snow was on its way. He is considered an expert on weather.

The Catts/Crawford family was nestled in their cabin for winter, firewood stacked high behind the cabin. The excitement of Christmas filled their thankful hearts. A new generation was started with baby Helen Frances. A letter from George and the Crawford boys assured everyone they were doing well. Jane Ann glanced around the room as she counted God's blessings one by one.

February 1838

I am secretly making Mama a new dress for her birthday. Since Charles's birthday is on Valentine's Day, I am making him some new overalls. Robert has gone with Papa to see the land he scouted out last year thirty miles west of here. Papa thinks the land will be good to grow apple trees.

Robert and Papa have more business at their law office than they can accomplish. Many more homesteaders are coming here to settle which keeps them busy.

As the town around the spring grows, Thomas and Robert use their skills to help establish the town. Mr. Campbell, the first landowner in the area named it. Built near a spring so settlers would have a good water source, he donated a fifty-acre field.

Robert filed the legal papers to incorporate the town which was known by the spring and was built in a field. All agreed the town would be called Springfield.

Robert served as one of the first trustees of the town. He was known as a man with deep faith in God and was highly respected as a lawyer. As he learned from his Uncle Charles, he wanted the rights of the state and the rights of the new community to be considered from the beginning of its establishment.

Summer 1838

Papa has found the land he wants to homestead in Lawrence County. He thinks they should move to the area and be first in line the day the land is released for homesteading. Within a few weeks, Robert and I helped them load their wagon which they will live in until an empty cabin becomes available.

We will stay in Springfield for now while Robert builds his law practice. I will miss Mama and Papa, but I am pleased to see they are getting closer to the dream they left Virginia to follow. Thomas L and Charles see the move as a new adventure.

I announced last night I am expecting another baby.

The most difficult challenge before Thomas and Frances in their trip to Lawrence County would be crossing Turnback Creek, with its deep drop offs on both sides. The drops prove to be most difficult for wagons. Many pioneers who were unsuccessful in attempting to cross in years past started calling it Turnback Creek—the point where they turned back toward Springfield.

Rolling their wagon west toward Mount Vernon, Thomas hoped to cross Turnback Creek before night fall. He thought if the good Lord were willing and the creek didn't rise, they'd try to cross.

Approaching the creek, Thomas took the reins sternly in his hands and called out to his mules, and the wagon moved slowly forward into the creek bed.

Thomas L and Charles whooped and hollered when they reached the other side. They were on their way to what Thomas called, "The Promise Land."

Late summer 1838

Mr. Fulbright travels to Lawrence County often by horseback. He drops by the cabin to see if I have anything to deliver to Mama and Papa. And he kindly brings back things from them. How nice it is to have our own delivery service. I show appreciation by having a warm blackberry cobbler for him to take home.

I miss Mama but am happy they are finally in Mount Vernon. She said she has never seen Papa so happy as when he showed her the land he thinks will grow the best apple trees. He is drawing up plans for the apple orchards, the house, and the barn. My heart sings to know they are happy. Now that they are living in a temporary cabin, we hope to go visit them soon.

Frances later shared with Jane Ann about the day Thomas took her and the boys to see the land. They walked the perimeter of the full one-hundred sixty acres to prayerfully dedicate the land to God and to call out for his blessings.

"Tired," she said, "I sat down under a huge oak tree so I could watch Thomas, Thomas L, and young

Charles make their plans for a new home—the Catts/
Crawford home on our own land."

Jane Ann later found a prayer her mother wrote
and had placed in the family Bible.

> Thank you, dear Lord, for fulfilling
> Thomas's dream to come west. It
> has been six long years since we first
> talked about homesteading land. We
> traveled over one-thousand miles
> and left some of our family behind
> to make this journey. With your
> provisions and protection, we are
> home on the land we will one day
> call our own. You, Lord, fill my heart
> and soul with overflowing joy to see
> Thomas so happy.
>
> Thank You Lord, for another good
> day.
>
> Frances Crawford, September 1, 1838

September 17, 1838

*I sit up, crying as I write in my diary. This morning I
looked out the kitchen window and saw Thomas L riding
at a fast gallop toward the cabin. Robert and I opened
the door, wondering what was wrong.*

*Tears were pouring down his face as he grabbed both of
our necks. Barely able to speak the words, he whispered,
"Papa died." I will never forget that painful moment as
I felt our strength drain from us.*

Sobbing, Robert grabbed his coat and saddlebag. Thomas

helped hitch up the mules while I got Helen Frances ready and packed our bag to leave. I felt I could not reach Mama soon enough. We both knew she needed us more now than ever before.

When we arrived, Mama was sitting beside his lifeless body in silence, still holding his hand. Charles and a neighbor, who offered to help, took Helen Frances to their cabin.

Robert and I sat with Mama. He softly said, "I will go make arrangements, Mama."

I watched Mama's tears fall one after another on Papa's lifeless hand. She looked at me and asked," What will I do without Thomas?" As she laid her head on my shoulder, I could feel her unbearable pain. She had again lost the man she loved.

I too asked God what we will all do without Papa. He was the strength and courage of our entire family. My heart breaks to imagine our family without him.

I must write a letter to George and my Crawford brothers to let them know our Papa has passed away. I know their hearts will be broken just as ours have been.

The unexpected death of Thomas Crawford once again brought pain to the Catts/Crawford family. It had been his dream to go west, but the dream was Thomas's, not Frances'. What would she do with two boys in a place that was not yet home for them? She would need to live in the cabin in town for at least a year before the land would be available to homestead. Should she stay or go back to Baltimore or Wellsburg?

As the oldest son, Robert assumed the responsibility to help his mother make decisions. First, he prayed for God's wisdom and comfort for his family.

A neighbor mentioned to Robert that perhaps Mr. Neely would allow his father to be buried in their family cemetery. Their farm was three miles west of where Thomas wanted to homestead land.

Many friends came from Springfield as the family gathered to bury Thomas, a man who was loved and respected by those who knew him.

They shared Frances's sadness in knowing Thomas's dream to homestead land lay in silence. Many friends asked one another, "What will Frances do without Thomas?"

CHAPTER 8

Late fall 1838

We stayed with Mama while Robert guided her through the difficult process of making decisions for her future. She wanted to go see the land once more before she decided on homesteading there.

I packed lunch while Thomas hitched the mules to the wagon.

As we pulled the wagon into the open field where Papa wanted to build a house, Mama's head fell into her hands and she sobbed. I heard her whisper to herself, "What will I do without Thomas?" She showed us where Papa wanted to plant the apple orchard and dreamed of one day building a church and school for future homesteaders.

Thomas L and Robert walked with Mama to the edge of the woods to see the tall oak trees Papa planned to cut for building his dream. Sitting on the wagon with Helen Frances and Charles, I watched as the colorful fall leaves drifted around them like a coat of many colors.

When they returned, Mama said, "I am going to fulfill your Papa's dream. We will homestead the land and stay in Missouri. God did not bring us one-thousand miles for me to give up. Nor did he bring us this far to leave us or to allow me to fail. We will go on with Thomas's plan."

My heart stopped for a moment. I could not imagine Mama homesteading the land with my two young brothers. I took her hands and looked into her eyes. I asked her if she was sure this is what she wanted.

With a smile, she nodded her head, and said, "Yes."

I assured her with God at our side, we would help her fulfil Papa's dream. Robert stepped over and put his arm around her shoulder. He promised her as a family we would be at her side.

The decision to remain in Missouri to homestead the land was a family decision. Robert and Thomas L pledged to help Frances as their Papa would have expected.

Robert and Jane Ann traveled back to their cabin in Springfield where he continued his work as the town lawyer. Young and determined, Thomas L accepted responsibility as the man of the house to do chores.

One afternoon while Thomas L was on his way home from getting supplies in Springfield, military soldiers ordered him to move his wagon to the side of the road. He did so and soon many Indian families march past him who were crying. Their tears touched him so deeply, he too cried.

Robert later explained to Thomas L about meeting Captain Clark, who wanted to see the families were treated fairly. However, not everyone saw the Indians as Captain Clark did. Their march became known as "The Trail of Tears."

Thomas L never forgot the sadness he felt as he watched the Indian families being forced to move. He often told the story about his blood brother,

Protector, who three times saved Charles's life. It seemed God had connected Thomas L's heart to the American Indians.

September 12, 1839

Mama laughingly told Robert she is going to sleep on the porch of the land office so she will be first in line to register the land Papa wanted. Robert plans to be there as her legal adviser.

Mama was proud to use Uncle John Neal's silver writing pen to sign the homestead paper. I thought of how proud Papa would be of Mama's determination to honor his dream. Thomas L made sure the sign our father carved was on the front of the wagon. He said Mama will need the words "In God Is Our Trust" more than ever.

Robert walked beside his Mama as she proudly exited the land office. She held her homestead claim high for everyone to see. The folks cheered as she walked past them. Perhaps she represented all the people who stepped out in faith to be American pioneers of the west. Or maybe that moment changed the lives of others who needed encouragement to follow their dream.

Jane Ann and Robert were concerned about their Mama's decision to live in the covered wagon—the same one they used to travel from Virginia. Thomas L and Charles passed the word around town they needed help building a cabin and barn next Saturday at the Catts/Crawford homestead.

Everyone, old and young, arrived at sunrise to help. They cut trees with whip saws and pilled them for the mules to drag them to where Frances wanted the cabin built. Large limbs were sawed to frame the windows and doors while others shaved shingles for roofing. The young men laughed when they were assigned to build the outhouse.

The ladies helped build two rope beds for the feather mattress they made as a housewarming gift. The men built a stall for the milk cow they gave as a gift.

Charles dug a bean hole for Jane Ann to cook the huge cast iron pot of beans for the workers. Robert made a spit big enough to roast the venison Thomas L shot in the woods. In appreciation to everyone, Frances made her special apple cobbler in an iron Dutch-oven on a wood fire.

The goat the Williams family loaned Frances to help chew down the brush had done a good job. Jane Ann, however, had never been near a goat. She learned the hard way not to bend over when a goat was around.

By sundown, the framing and roofing on the cabin was finished. The brush and limbs were piled high for a bonfire. Frances, Thomas L, Charles, Robert, Jane Ann, and Helen Frances stepped up on the porch of the new cabin to thank everyone. Preacher Nordyke stepped up to pray God's blessing to be with the Catts/Crawford family.

Immediately after he said, "Amen," Charles started taping his foot and clapping his hands. Thomas L picked up his fiddle and started to play. Around and around everyone danced to celebrate a good day.

Later, totally exhausted, everyone fell asleep with a thankful heart, knowing Thomas Crawford's dream had come true.

September 1839

I am on my knees to pray as my mama taught me, and I will write out my prayer so I will never forget this day and remember to always pray this prayer for them.

Dear Lord, you have brought us full circle. Papa's dream is fulfilled. Please give mama, Thomas L, and Charles strength to live on the land when they are weak. Give them courage when they are afraid. Give them hope when they are discouraged. Teach them to trust you as their shield of protection. Give them your blessing as they serve you in this new place they call home.

Thank you, God, for another good day. Amen

Spring 1840

I am thankful Mama traveled to Springfield to help me with the delivery of our second baby. Labor was hard and long as our baby boy was born breech, feet first. I was exhausted but still wanted to hold our precious John Thomas Catts/Crawford. We named him in honor of my father, John Catts and our Papa, Thomas Crawford. As I did with Helen Frances I wanted to count his toes and his fingers. I wanted to look at his face to see God's amazing creation. All Robert wanted to do was to hold his baby boy and dance around the room. After such a difficult delivery, Mama insisted I stay in bed for several days to heal. She trusted Thomas L and Charles could manage things at the farm while she was away.

Thinking perhaps they might need some help and since Jane Ann was getting good care from her mama, Robert left at sunup and rode by horseback to Mount Vernon. As he headed up the trail to the cabin, he saw an unusual sight. Wooden cages were lined up next to the barn. Charles was busy going from cage to cage.

As he rode closer, he saw Charles was holding up a big black snake. Hesitant as he climbed down from his horse, Robert questioned what he was doing. Charles returned the snake to the bucket and laid a board and heavy rock on top.

Turning to Robert, Charles proudly said, "I am catching animals so I can sell them. Every homesteader will need a black snake for their barn. They keep the rats and mice away."

Thomas L came out of the barn. The two older brothers walked along talking as they inspected Charles's animal collection. He had quail, rabbits, two good size turkeys, a wash tub full of bullfrogs and a bucket with two black snakes curled inside. Not impressed, Robert walked around the side of the barn.

Before Thomas L or Charles could warn him, Robert received a double shot of skunk spay.

Yelling and mad, Robert stomped into the barn where he stripped off his clothes. Thomas L hurried to the house to start water boiling. Charles pushed over the horse trough and started pumping clean water into it.

Looking around to see if anyone could see him, Robert ran from the barn to the horse trough and climbed in. No one said a word. Thomas L brought a pot of hot water and a big jug of cider vinegar to pour into the trough.

Not cracking a smile, all Robert could do was sit still and hope the vinegar would take away the skunk smell. Thomas L and Charles dragged a work bench from the barn to sit on. All three sat looking at each other, not saying a word.

Robert started robustly laughing and said, "After two years at West Point, years of studying law, here I sit, skunked!"

Thomas L and Charles hesitantly laughed with him.

They sat all afternoon with Robert soaking in the cider vinegar. Thomas L thought it best to bury Roberts's clothes in the dirt for at least a week or maybe two, hoping to get rid of the skunk smell.

When Robert returned home the next day wearing Thomas L's old, worn out clothes, Jane Ann detected a skunk smell. Neither she nor Frances asked what happened. They thought it best to wait until Robert was ready to tell his story.

Late summer 1840

Mama is upset she misplaced the letter from George telling her he and Mary Ann had married. I showed her a letter I received letting us know they have a baby girl they named Mary Frances. With so many Frances's in the family, they want to call her "Fannie."

Each time I write to him, I remind him he promised one day to move to Missouri. And how much fun our children could have growing up together.

George and Mary Ann purchased part ownership in the mercantile in Wellsburg, Virginia. The Crawford brothers wrote to inform everyone the apple orchards will have a bountiful harvest. They continued to send a share of the orchard profits to Frances, Robert, and Thomas L. They saved Charles's part for when he'd turn twenty-one.

Thomas L is continuing to work with Mr. Henson to become a wheelwright. Wagons and stagecoaches would be a means of transportation for many years. He felt it was a good trade to learn for the future.

Jane Ann and Robert bought land in both Springfield and Mount Vernon. Now that he was a circuit lawyer, he travelled by horseback to court and continue to build his law practice in Springfield—Crawford and Wilson, Attorneys at Law.

Spring 1841

Robert and I go to the farm to help Mama as often as we can. Thomas L has worked all winter cutting the standing hardwood oak trees on the farm to finish Mama's house. He will follow the plans Papa drew before his passing. I think Thomas L, now twenty-four years old, feels since he is not married, it is his responsibility to take care of Mama. I pray he will not place his future on hold. He needs to feel the love of a good wife and have a family of his own.

Irritated with me, he said, "I will ask for your advice, big sister, when it is needed." There is nothing like brotherly love.

On my next visit, I will bring Thomas L potato candy or a chocolate pie topped with calf slobbers, as it is called in Missouri. I laugh at the difference in what things are called. In Virginia and Baltimore, we called calf slobbers meringue.

With my special surprise, perhaps Thomas L will not stay mad at me.

Piles of sawed lumber were stacked in four directions for Thomas L to conveniently use to build a new house. He kept ten-year-old Charles busy and out of the way by giving him the chore of counting boards and organizing supplies.

Thomas L took on many responsibilities when his Papa died and most likely never had time to grieve for the only Papa he ever really knew. Perhaps building the house was a way he could honor the love he had for Thomas Crawford.

The Fulbright family often stopped by to help Thomas L. Mrs. Fulbright often brought Frances flower bulbs and starts for her flower garden. Sharing seeds and plants was part of being neighborly.

Long, hot summer 1841

At the end of a long day, I questioned why I thought we wanted to move to Missouri. I had no idea of the great number of chiggers and ticks that live here. Now that they have made my body their home, I can uncomfortably take a wild guess.

JUST A MOMENT

I consider it a blessing I did not experience a snake bite while picking wild strawberries along the creek. I guess I can repeat what an old farmer in town told me, "I live above the snakes." He laughs and assures me it means as long as he is above ground, he is still alive.

I am puzzled why so many giant June bugs occupy the blackberry bushes in the woods. When I reach to pick the berries, they make a startling buzzing sound and fly toward my face. Sometimes I just cannot understand life in Missouri. I am confused why anyone wants to pick gooseberries to make pies or jelly. It takes twice as much sugar to sweeten the tiny, sour, green balls.

Caring for two little ones and another on the way while trying to gather or grow food is exhausting. If I close my eyes and try really hard, I can remember walking with Mama down Lexington Street to the Lexington Market to buy our fresh fruits and vegetables. I envision myself reaching to choose which of the beautiful fruits from around the world I want to purchase.

I am suddenly awakened from my daydreams by the sound of a baby crying. I open my eyes to reality. I chose to be a pioneer woman. I remind myself I am thankful Robert and Thomas L hunt for our wild meats, smoke them, and wring the chicken's necks for me to cook. With that thought in mind, I am a blessed woman. But oh, how I miss Aunt Lois's chicken and dumplings and Ms. Thelma's berry pies. Not to mention the sweet Winesap apple pies Mama made from the apples in our Virginia orchards.

I have finished emptying my heart of my complaints. The children are asleep, Robert is at a town meeting, and I am tired. I will retreat to the swing Robert hung on the porch. Here I will let my mind rest while I watch the lightening bugs. As the day draws to an end, the warm golden colors of a sunset are as wide as the ocean. I bow my head, ashamed of my complaining.

Life was hard for those who moved west from big cities. There they had rose garden courtyards. Here they pushed an iron plow pulled by a mule. With a shovel they dug holes to plant seeds. Then they prayed for God to send soaking rains to grow what they planted. They picked and harvested their gardens and crops, canned, and dried foods and then celebrated because they had enough provisions for winter.

Their work was never done. And they always had to be prepared for the unexpected.

Grams looked at Lydia and smiled. Her reading was improving as she learned about history and the family buried in the farm's hay field. "Would you like to hear a prayer my friend Mrs. Baker taught me?"

"Yes please," Lydia said, nodding.

Grams bowed her head. "Holy Spirit, show yourself in my life. Let me breathe your breath, see with your eyes, feel with your feelings, think with your thoughts, speak your words and hear your voice." She looked up. "That's a prayer we can all pray when we feel overwhelmed like Jane Ann felt."

Lydia nodded in agreement with Grams. "I understand why Jane Ann wanted to keep working on her reading," she said. "The more times I see a word, the easier it is for me to memorize."

"You've definitely made progress," Grams said. "I'm proud of you. The more you understand about being dyslexic, the more you can help yourself."

They all said goodnight, and Grams fell asleep, grateful for her family and for sweet Lydia. She looked forward to each new day in seeing her build confidence and excitement to learn.

BEAN-HOLE BEANS

12 Cups of pinto beans, white beans, or soldier's beans
1 ½ lbs of salt pork or Applewood bacon
2 large sweet onions
3 Cups of molasses or brown sugar
½ Cup dry spicy mustard
¾ Cup of butter
3 Tbs chili powder if desired

Dig a three-foot deep hole two and a half foot across. Be sure it is big enough for your cast iron bean pot to go down into hole with six inches to spare around the edge. Layer rocks in the bottom to help hold the heat while the beans cook. Broken clay pots will also hold the heat.

Layer dry hardwood such as oak on top of the rocks almost to the top of the hole and carefully start the fire. Let it burn for several hours to make good hot coals. While fire is burning, put beans in a large pot on the stove covered in water to boil. Cook for about an hour. Check to see if the skin on the beans will roll back when you blow on them. Don't overcook.

Cut salt pork into strips about ¼ inch thick. Place it in the bottom of the pot along with sliced onions. Pour the beans and the broth into the pot. Add molasses, dry mustard and salt and pepper. Add chunks of butter and more water. Place heavy duty aluminum foil over the top of the pot and press down the edges to hold the heat. Put the lid on pot as tight as possible.

With a shovel, remove one-third of the coals from the bean hole. Put to pile to the side of the hole or on a piece of metal. Very carefully put the bean pot in the hole on top of the remaining coals. With a shovel, add the coals around the cast iron bean pot. Then cover the top of the pot with coals. Use the dirt from where you dug the hole to mound on top of the hole. Place a piece of tin or an old tarp on top with rocks or bricks to hold it down.

Let the beans cook all night. Dig the bean hole out and remove the bean-hole pot. Carefully remove the lid so not to be steamed. Salt and pepper to your taste and serve with cornbread sticks and red peppers.

Usually Bean-Hole Beans were cooked for a workday or when pioneers planned to stay somewhere for several says. Travelers on wagon trains often dug a bean-hole as soon as they stopped for the night so they would have beans cooked for the next day.

TATE'S CHOCOLATE CREAM PIE WITH CALF SLOBBERS

¾ stick of butter melted in a large skillet (pioneers called butter cow grease)

In a covered container or jar, shake the following ingredients:

3 Cups milk

¼ Cup flour

1 ½ Cups sugar

5 egg yolks, beaten. (save the egg whites)

3 Tbs cocoa

Shake until smooth. Pour into skillet with butter.

Cook until thick and creamy. Add 1 Tbs real vanilla.

Pour into large baked pie crust.

While pie is cooling make the calf slobbers.

Calf Slobbers

5 Egg whites

Beat at high speed with a mixer or eggbeater in a glass bowl until frothy. Peaks should easily form with a spoon.

Add:

1 Tbs vanilla

½ tsp cream of tarter

3 Tbs sugar

Continue to beat with the mixer or eggbeater until peaks form. Spoon calf slobbers on top of chocolate filling.

Bake at 350 degrees for 10 minutes or until golden brown.

Cool and serve.

Pioneers called meringue, "Calf Slobbers," because it looked like the stiff foam that forms around a calf's mouth when he sucks his mama's milk.

CHAPTER 9

December 6, 1841

We planned a surprise birthday party for Thomas L. He has worked endlessly to finish Mama's house so they can move in the first of December and be settled before Christmas. Not everything is done inside, but he can work on those things when there is snow on the ground. He has chopped firewood for the winter, and Charles has piled it in stacks. All the filled canning jars, bushel baskets of potatoes, and fruits are packed away in the root cellar until needed. Even the barn and corrals are finished. His work has not gone unnoticed. Robert and I noticed.

A horse farmer named Werner and his wife, Sherry, needed Robert to do some legal work for him. He was unable to pay him. He offered to instead give Robert any horse he wanted in his corral. Robert chose a solid black stallion.

When he showed me the horse, I remembered how handsome Robert looked when he came home from West Point Military Academy. He was riding a black stallion across the green field, and I knew then I was in love with him. I was so pleased he would again have a black stallion.

He hugged me and said, "It is not mine to keep. I think you will agree with who we can give the horse to as a gift."

Neighbors and friends coming for a visit on a cold December day, and Robert and Jane Ann coming to stay for the weekend should have given Thomas L a clue that something was up. He hadn't even noticed the dishpan turned upside down on the table on the back porch. Everyone knew that is where birthday cakes were kept. He most likely hadn't given one thought about it being his birthday. He'd been so busy trying to settle his Mama in the new house before Christmas, he was too tired to notice.

He had been in the woods searching for a lost cow most of the morning. Tired and cold, he opened the door to hear Jane Ann yell, "Surprise!"

Thomas L was definitely surprised. Humbled and embarrassed, he lowered his head and took a seat by the warm fire. His friends and family presented him with many gifts of appreciation. Feasting and celebrating for Thomas L continued most of the afternoon.

After everyone was gone, Robert asked him to show him the new barn. When he pushed open the barn door, he saw a beautiful, solid black stallion horse tied to a post.

Robert walked over and rubbed the horse's back. Looking at Thomas L, he said, "This is a gift from Jane Ann and me."

Thomas L was speechless. He looked down at the ground for a moment then raised his head, looked at his brother, and smiled from ear to ear. Overwhelmed with gratitude, he put his arm around Roberts shoulder, and asked, "Can I take him for a ride?"

While they saddled up the beautiful stallion, they agreed to name him "Ira." Thomas L climbed up on his birthday gift and first rode past the house so everyone could see him. Then he rode through the snow-covered fields with the ice-cold wind blowing against him. He later said it was a ride he would never forget.

Spring 1842

My dear Robert thinks he can help everyone. Being a circuit court attorney keeps him traveling from town to town. He gets upset when an injustice is served on someone he knows is innocent. I remind him Uncle Charles taught him to never disrespect or argue with a judge.

Mama has given him some Scriptures from the Bible to memorize. She suggested he use these Scriptures as a base for his argument whenever he gets upset in court. She said, "God's Word will win every time."

At the time, judges were often unfair and perhaps crooked. A money pouch stuck under the cushion on the Judge's chair or "bench" as it was called, could easily determine the outcome of a trial.

Robert not only often disagreed with the Judge but also the prosecuting attorney. Once when a wealthy banker from Saint Louis tried to take a poor farmer's land due to an error in the deed, Robert became very upset. Knowing the judge had been bribed, his anger overcame him. He punched the attorney and accused the judge of being paid to make his decision. Robert was fined ten dollars for contempt of court.

January 1843

Mama is grieving once again. Robert personally delivered a Saint Louis newspaper to her. She read the headline out loud, "Francis Scott Key, Author of the Star-Spangled Banner, died in Baltimore, Maryland, January 11, 1843."

"Oh, say can you see by the dawn's early light," Lydia began to sing. "Did Frances Crawford really know Francis Scott Key?"

"According to family stories and conformation by historians, yes, she did. Even her obituary stated she'd been personal friends with him," Grams said. "And a historian, who thought more than likely she did receive a piece of the Star-Spangled Banner flag, confirmed it."

"Wow! I can't imagine being given something so important as a piece of the most famous flag in American history." Lydia replied.

Grams suggest they take a break and have some cold lemonade on the porch.

Lydia and Pops sat in the porch swing watching the humming birds buzz from one feeder to the next. The redbirds stopped at the feeders Pops hung from the low branches of the old cedar tree in the corner of the yard

They peacefully swung back and forth, watching the birds and listening to the squeaking chain on the swing.

Lydia asked Pops, "Why don't you fix the squeak in the chain?"

"It's one of the reasons I love this old place, Lydia," Pops replied. "It's the sound of being home."

Since Frances Neal Catts/Crawford's family lived in Baltimore and the Key family lived within traveling distance, the families were good friends. Many people in the area thought the families might be friends. This was confirmed when Frances's brother, John Neal, was a member of the Delphine Poet Writer Society as was Francis Scott Key. The two of them helped establish the exclusive club that allowed only nine members at a time.

Even though he was older than Frances, he most likely entertained the younger children while their parents talked politics or enjoyed visiting. He often quoted Shakespeare from the balcony of his parent's home at Tara Rubra.

"What is in a name? A rose by any name would smell as sweet," (Romeo and Juliet Act 2, Scene 2).

Young Frances attended his wedding to Mary Taylor Lloyd, whom he affectionately called Ms. Polly. Frances sneezed while at their wedding, so he gave her his handkerchief with his initials, F. S. K. They stayed in touch for many years.

Summer 1844

Our house is finished in Mount Vernon I am excited to be closer to family. It seems foolish to have another house in Springfield, but Robert needs a resting place after many long hours of court in Springfield. He keeps his law books there so he can study them at night.

I enjoy being closer to the Catts/Crawford farm so I can spend time with Mama. I love to sit on the front porch with her, look out over the land, and watch our children play.

I sometimes wonder how the farm would look if Papa had lived. Thomas L does a fine job, but Papa had such big dreams. I think he would have persevered to establish the apple orchard. He would be proud of Thomas L for accepting the responsibility to manage and work the farm and to care for Mama and Charles. And I know Papa would be proud of Robert as a well-respected attorney. As much as Charles likes animals, Papa most likely would have taught him to raise fine horses. Perhaps he would be proud of me as well, the city gal who became a pioneer woman.

If only Papa had lived. Robert has his eyes and looks like him. I see Mama lovingly pat his face like she did Papa. Thomas L has Papa's laugh. And Charles has Papa's heart of adventure. Robert said I have our Papa's strong and yet soft, caring heart. I hope so. To have Mama's heart of compassion and Papa's strong, soft heart, I am honored.

Jane Ann didn't often sit and think about the "if-only's" in her life. She stayed busy making a home and caring for four children. She became a care-giver to all family and friends. Excellent at sewing for her family, when time allowed, she made hats. Her Grandmother Neal's silver thimble was always in use.

The Great Migration West, as it was called, on the Oregon Trail caught the attention of all Americans. By the end of his term, President James K Polk wanted the United States to stretch from coast to coast. Protestant missionaries hoping to further Christianity in the west were the first people in wagons to cross the Continental Divide. Thousands of wagons followed, each loaded with a pioneer's dreams.

For some time, Thomas L had been considering going on the Oregon Trail. The following spring, he headed to Independence, Missouri to be a wheelwright for a wagon train outfit.

April 1, 1845

We had a bittersweet celebration last night for Thomas L before he leaves to travel on the Oregon Trail. I have always looked at him as my younger brother who I needed to protect. Now I see him as a strong, courageous man who protected each of us after Papa died. As much as I want to discourage him, I instead hope he will blaze the trail of his dreams with the prayers our family will lay before and behind him.

I know if he does not go now, he will never go. As painful as it is to tell him goodbye, I am thankful it is his time to become the man God is calling him to be. I will miss him as I do George. I pray one day God will bring our family together again in one place.

Jane Ann and Frances were determined to not let Thomas L see them cry. He had seen and heard them cry since he was a little boy whenever heartache struck their lives. This time they wanted him to remember their smiles instead of their tears.

Robert helped Thomas L prepare Ira, his black stallion, to be ready for the trail. Using his West Point training, he made sure Thomas L would be fully equipped for travel, checking his saddle to be sure it fit like an old rocking chair, saddle bags properly packed, and canteen filled. And making sure he had the silver compass given to him by Uncle John Neal. As tough as both Robert and Thomas L were, they would still be sad to say goodbye to each other.

Charles and Frances would be the most difficult to leave behind. Before mounting his horse, Thomas L gave them both one last hug and whispered to his Mama, "I left you a gift, but you have to find it."

Thomas L pointed Ira, his black stallion, north toward Independence. Slapping the horse's rump with the reins, he rode off in a fast gallop, never looking back.

This one moment changed Thomas L's life.

Knowing Thomas L loved walking in the woods. Frances thought perhaps that was where she might find the gift he mentioned. She took long walks most every day, searching for his gift.

Early one morning when the citrus-smelling white blooms of the May apples hovered above the ground in the woods, Frances found her gift. The morning sun was like a light from heaven shinning directly down on a cross carved in the stump of a tree. Tears welled up in her eyes as she reverently approached a wooden cross. She bowed to her knees and prayed for her son. The cross would become her resting place for many years to come.

July 4, 1845

Independence Day is my favorite time to celebrate and be thankful we are a free nation. This year we will have a double celebration. Today, Mount Vernon is established as our county seat. Robert has promised to take me to the dance after the fireworks. Some think it will last all night.

We are happy to be near Mama and Charles while Thomas L travels west. She hopes every day to receive a letter from him. I remind her, towns to drop off or pick up mail are far and few between.

To celebrate Mount Vernon being established as the county seat, people came from all over Lawrence County to join the celebration. The county was named in honor of the gallant sea captain, James Lawrence, whose last words were, "Don't give up the ship."

The town of Mount Vernon was named after President George Washington's beloved home place, Mount Vernon, Virginia.

JUST A MOMENT

Christmas 1845

I watched out the window as the cold north wind blew in a snowstorm a few days before Christmas. Thomas L wrote Mama a letter saying he would be home for Christmas. I wondered if he was caught in the storm. Mama wanted us to all be together when he arrived home. We loaded our wagon and faced the brutal storm to drive three miles to the farm. Robert wrapped the children in quilts and tucked another one over the top to shield them from the snow.

When we arrived at the farm, I sensed Mama was worried about Thomas L. After waiting a long while, we tucked the children into bed and waited with Mama by the fire. Tired, Robert and I finally retired for the evening.

The sound of Mama's voice woke me up. I got out of bed and tiptoed to the hearth room where I could hear her calling out to God to bring Thomas L home safely. As she ended her prayer in the stillness of the night, I thought I could hear a sound coming from the north field. I listened. It sounded like someone riding a horse. With every step the horse took, I could hear the frozen snow crunch. Suddenly, it stopped. A man stomped up on the porch and banged loudly on the door. Mama and I looked at each other and went to the door.

Robert had been awakened, rushed into the hearth room, and motioned for me and Mama to move back away from the door. Quickly grabbing the shotgun that rested at the side of the hearth, he yanked the door open with the gun in hand. There stood Thomas L, covered in snow. The answer to Mama's prayer was home for Christmas.

For weeks, the entire family was glued to every word Thomas L shared about his travels west.

Many were about the beautiful country he saw. He described the sound of a buffalo stampede, the smell of mountain flowers, and the taste of water from a cold, rushing stream. He also explained the inscriptions carved on enormous rocks. Many carvings were simply a name and a date; others were Scriptures from God's Word. He assured us he would never be able to explain how beautiful God's creation was on the trail west.

Thomas L would leave again in spring to travel west with the wagon train.

Fall 1846

Mama asked me to walk with her to the cross in the woods. I had never seen her gift from Thomas L. I enjoyed the time with her so much. The gold and red leaves slowly drifted around us to find their resting place. I tried to imagine the gold leaves falling from the tall aspen trees in Colorado Thomas L had described to us.

The rustling sound of the fallen leaves reminded me of walking in the apple orchards in Virginia. I thought about George and Mary Ann, his wife none of us had ever met. Mama hasn't seen George in twelve years. I patted the tiny baby inside of me, thinking how hard it would be to not see your child for so many years.

Through the trees, I could see the cross in front of us, so I let Mama go on ahead to give her time to pray. I took paper and a pencil from my apron pocket wrote down names of those I love. I tore them apart and threw them up into the air. A swirling fall wind blew at that moment. The names on the papers flew upward as if they were being

delivered to God in heaven. Only God can orchestrate a
perfect moment I will never forget.

Like Frances, Jane Ann was dedicated to praying for her family. When she wrote on the paper, she whispered their names to God.

December 1847

Now that Thomas L is home for Christmas, Robert thinks
we should write a letter to George. Together, we should
ask him when he is going to fulfill his promise to Mama.
His promise was to move to Missouri after he found a
nice Virginia gal to marry.

Charles, now sixteen, hung on every word Thomas L told him about traveling on the Oregon Trail. Robert feared Mama would one day need to let go of another son to westward travel.

Much had changed back east as in the west. Samuel F. B. Morse showed off his telegraph the previous year by sending a message from the chambers of the Supreme Court in Washington D. C. to Baltimore. A new era in communication began with the words, "What hath God wrought?"

Only a year later, Boston was connected to New York by telegraph wire. Mail service was also improving. The first U. S. postage stamps were available for sale in New York City.

And Hanson Gregory created the best new food—the first ring doughnut.

Summer 1848

I think I would like to stop time. Our children are growing up so fast, and the world wants to snatch them away from me. The influence society has on young people is not good. The gold rush in California seems to have brought out the worst in people. Thomas L said in his last letter that greed and lawlessness is filling communities in the west. Claim jumping and robbery are common.

Robert sees it happening here as well. Farmers develop feuds that last for years. In one case which preceded to court, the men could not remember why they were feuding. I pray God will stop the growing darkness of evil and shine his glorious light into people's hearts.

Thomas L received a letter from his wagon master asking him to report to the wagon train one month early. Confident in his skills, Wagon Master Summers asked him to become a scout for the train. His wife would be traveling with the train. To entice Thomas L, he promised Mrs. Summers would make apple dumplings for him once a week. Thomas L considered the opportunity a great honor.

Gold was discovered in California. The trails were overcome with racing wagons filled with folks wanting to search for gold. Robert thought he should saddle up his horse and head west. With five children, perhaps he felt like Jane Ann—a little tied down with responsibilities.

November 1849

I am proud of Robert for the fine job he is doing as an attorney. He is only thirty-seven years old and has been asked to consider running for the Missouri Senate, but for now, he has declined. He wants to be home as much as possible to teach our children. I notice him laying his law books aside and reading to the children from his Bible. We both agree if God's Word is not woven in a growing heart, God will be forgotten. "The Book of Knowledge," is the living Word of God that will never leave them. For myself, the Scriptures where I filled in my name, are in my heart forever.

I remember Mama telling me, "God fills a mother's heart with unending love for her children."

I agree.

Jane Ann's friend Linda gave her words to pray for her children. "God, I ask you to give our children a heart that never hardens but instead stays soft and open to your leading. Protect them from a temper of anger and instead allow your love to never fail and to overflow from them. And give them a soft touch that will never hurt anyone but instead a hand to give love and compassion."

More memories were made at the Catts/Crawford Christmas dinner table. Thomas L, Robert, Jane Ann, and this time Charles, all wrote a letter to George asking when he will move to Missouri. They kept it a secret from Frances.

Spring 1850

Robert and I have been spending time with Thomas L before he leaves with the wagon train. While sitting on the porch last night watching Mama playing games with the children, we talked about the memories of when our families became one. I asked Robert and Thomas L if they remembered our ride in the red, horse-drawn sleigh in Baltimore.

Robert laughed and immediately said, "It was my idea. I suggested if Papa wanted to impress Mrs. Catts, he should take her on a sleigh ride in the snow. And if he really wanted to impress her, he should take all the kids." Thomas L robustly laughed out loud.

Charles joined us on the porch and wanted to hear more about the sleigh ride. As we talked, Robert said, "Let's do it again. We can build our own Catts/Crawford red sleigh."

I noticed Thomas L and Charles raised their eyebrows with interest.

For now, it is just talk, but perhaps if I keep reminding them, we will have the sleigh built by the time George moves to Missouri.

Leaning back in our chairs, sitting quietly we watching the children run around the yard playing. They were being kids as we had once been. Such sweet memories I hang on to.

The seed had been planted. Perhaps a sleigh really could be built. The iron runners and iron frame would take a long time to build. While Thomas L was away, Robert said he would inquire about getting the iron work done at Mr. Pyle's blacksmith shop. Their friend, Mr. Miller had built many sleighs. He offered to look at the drawings when they're finished.

While sitting by the campfire at night on the trail, Thomas L sketched plans for the sleigh. Charles cut and dried the lumber to be ready to work on when Thomas L returned. Jane Ann would keep everyone encouraged to do their part. They all agreed it would be a surprise for their Mama.

Christmas 1850

I made good use of Grandma Neal's silver thimble again this year. It seems all of the children needed new coats or an extra quilt for their bed. Now that Robert has more responsibility in the community, it seems I am always making him a new white shirt. After seeing several children in raggedy clothes running around town, I started a ladies' sewing circle to make clothes of all sizes. Once a month we prepare a meal for those in need and let them pick out new clothes. This makes my heart sing with joy. Robert reminded me of my prayer to have a heart like Mama.

For some reason, I have started having trouble with my reading again. The letters seem to move as they did when I was a child. I will try to spend more time concentrating on my reading, hoping to improve my problem once again. When I do my daily Bible reading, I will double the chapters and read more slowly to see if that helps. I have learned concentration is important.

I started writing a Christmas story for our children this year. It began,

"Christmas time was very near, and oh what a glorious time of year.

To be at Grandma's house for Christmas is ..."

I began making Christmas gifts and never finished the story.

After our Christmas dinner together at the farm, the story of the Bethlehem Star and reading from the Bible, I thought about the Christmas story I had not finished. As we sat watching the warm, twinkling fire, I was disappointed in myself for not finishing. Suddenly, I thought that the children could each create their own Christmas story about spending time with Mama.

I started with the youngest and said, "Christmas time was very near, and oh what a glorious time of year. To be at Grandma's house for Christmas is ..." and let them complete the story.

We had so much fun.

Each child, one after another, told his or her own story about being with Grandma at Christmas. Even Robert, Jane Ann, and Thomas L shared stories they remembered about their Grandma Neal. Frances had the most interesting stories about her grandma who came to America from London.

The unfinished Christmas story became another family tradition with the Catts/Crawford family.

"Grams, do you think I'll always have trouble reading?" Lydia asked.

"You might, Lydia. But like me, you could work on your reading every day. That's how I fell in love with reading and learning. The more I read, the easier it became and the more I learned." Grams smiled thoughtfully.

"And you still want to learn about Jane Ann Crawford, don't you? How about you read for a while?" Lydia added.

Grams nodded as Lydia started to hand the antique diary to her. Hesitating, Lydia said, "I never thought I would like to read about someone's life I don't know. But I'm learning many things from Jane Ann that I would never have known."

"That's right, Lydia," Pops chimed in. "You're learning history through the Catts/Crawford family. They lived history every day. They lived in the past; we live in the present and future. One day, maybe someone will read your diary as history."

Thinking about what Pops said, Lydia's smile beamed as she listened to Grams continue reading.

CHAPTER 10

Early spring 1851

I am so happy and excited the plans are finalized to build a red Christmas sleigh for Mama. Before leaving to go back on the trail, Thomas L finished the work with Mr. Pyle, the blacksmith, on the iron runners and the frame. He secretly delivered the parts in his wagon. For now, Charles can hide the metal work in the barn until needed. He and Robert have selected the best oak trees to cut for the lumber to build the sleigh. They think the wood will be dry by the time Thomas L returns in late fall.

George and Mary Ann are making plans to leave Virginia by mid-summer so they can arrive here before winter winds blow with snow. She is expecting a baby, so travel, as I well know, will be slow. I am so thankful we will soon be together. They will not only be here for Christmas but also for Mama, Charles, and George's birthdays in February.

Travel across country with a large family hadn't changed much since the rest of the Catts/Crawford family moved west. Trains and riverboats connected large cities. However, Old Man River, as the Mississippi River was called, kept rolling along to be the main obstacle for pioneers to cross. Ferries stayed busy bringing wagons across until years later when the world's first steel bridge was built.

At the time, one in four bridges failed with disastrous results. Eads Bridge was built to make access to the west easier. Andrew Carnegie, a visionary steel manufacturer, knew people had to be confident in bridges before they'd use them. For that reason, an elephant was brought in to test the safety of Eads Bridge. They were certain an elephant wouldn't walk across foundations that were unstable due to their natural instincts. After the elephant walked across, Eads Bridge became an open door to the west.

December 1851

George's family arrived safely to Mount Vernon. Unknown to Mama, they are staying hidden away at our house until Christmas Eve. I love George's wife, Mary Ann, and their children. She had an early, difficult delivery with their new baby, Clarence. I feel a little sad we are not letting Mama know George is in town. Even so, they need rest after their long trip so they can enjoy seeing her later.

Our surprise sleigh is ready and in the barn. Thomas L stayed up half the night adding the last coat of red paint. I asked Mama to crochet hats and gloves for our family, as our Christmas gifts, and I have crocheted some for George's family. Everyone will have new hats and gloves for our surprise sleigh ride.

Robert and I are busy cooking not only for our guests but also for our traditional Christmas dinner. Charles feels like a turkey with his head cut off, running around doing whatever needs to be done.

Nothing could be more fun than the surprise we have

planned for our Mama. She has guided us through so many difficult times with love and compassion while she was hurting more than anyone knew. Together, we will make this her best Christmas ever.

As soon as Thomas L returned from the trail, he started working on the sleigh. Robert, Charles, and he spent late nights in the barn sanding and smoothing the wood. They anxiously waited for two warm nights to paint the sleigh. Robert made the sign, "Catts/Crawford Family," which he'd attach to the back. Charles gathered red berries, pine sprigs, and greenery to make garland to decorate the sleigh. They would attach black oil lanterns on the front corners to guide the sleigh into the night.

Jane Ann's job was to take care of George's family and pray for God to let it snow on Christmas Eve.

Christmas Eve 1851

I will sit down a few moments to rest. I am exhausted, and Mama is mad. She thinks we have taken over her kitchen and her house. Robert explained to her, "You need to rest, Mama."

Later she will forgive us, but for now, she thinks we are taking charge. She is upset with me for making the Sweet Milk Sugar Cookies for Christmas morning. If only she knew how many I had to make to have enough for George's family. I am keeping an eye on the ticking mantel clock. It is almost time for George to arrive. Back to the kitchen I must go.

As the clock struck six, everyone listened. Jane Ann went to the bedroom to peek out the window to see if they were coming up the road. She watched as the glittering snow silently fell. Bowing her head, she whispered, "Thank you, dear God, for letting us bring joy to our Mama tonight and for bringing George home to us."

As she raised her head, she heard the sound of horses pulling a wagon through the frozen snow. She hurried back to the hearth room to wait.

Suddenly, the sound of footsteps coming up the porch steps could be heard, followed by voices and a loud knock at the door.

Robert said, "You should open the door, Mama."

When Frances cautiously opened the door, George, leaning forward, softly said, "Merry Christmas, Mama."

Frances fell into her son's arms. "Oh, George, I've missed you so much."

He turned with an open arm and said, "I want you to meet my wife, Mary Ann, and your grandchildren."

Frances lowered her head as tears fell to the floor. She mumbled, "Thank you, God. After seventeen years our family is finally back together." Trying her best to smile, she stretched her arms around George, Mary Ann, and their six children. As she hugged each one, they told her their names.

Then George helped Mary Ann take off her wool cape, revealing a baby wrapped in blankets in her arms. "And this is baby Clarence," he said.

Frances held him while Mary Ann and George's family warmed themselves by the fire.

After a bountiful Christmas dinner, everyone knew it was time for the Bethlehem Star story and the reading of the Christmas story from God's Word. The children quietly sat down on the rag rug in front of the cozy fire and the adults pulled up chairs behind them.

Stepping forward, Thomas L picked up the apple. Turning toward Charles, he handed him the apple and said, "It is your turn, little brother."

Surprised by his brother's passing of the tradition, Charles proudly stood up and accepted the apple. He showed the children how to slice the apple sideways, so they could see the star in the center of the sliced apple.

He explained how God had placed a star in every apple to remind us about the star that shinned bright over Bethlehem the night Jesus was born.

Charles added, "May God keep each of us as the apple of his eye and in his care."

After Charles finished, Robert picked up the family Bible and carefully turned the pages to Luke 2. As he stood up, tears filled his eyes and fell upon the pages. He looked at his brother George and said with a quivering voice, "It's your turn. That's how Papa would want it."

Tears filled George's eyes as he humbly accepted the Bible. With honor, he proudly started reading, "And it came to pass..."

The family continued sitting by the crackling, warm fire, sharing past memories and the children making new ones. No one noticed Thomas L and Charles slip out the back door.

Soon, sounds were heard in front of the house.

Somewhat confused, Frances asked, "Is that Christmas carols and bells I hear?" She quickly crossed the room and cautiously opened the door. Peeking outside, she was totally surprised to see a beautiful red Christmas sleigh, abundantly decorated with garland, red berries, large red bows, and two black oil lanterns to light the way. Two horses with pine wreaths hanging around their neck were hitched to the sleigh.

Sitting in the sleigh with an obvious glee of excitement on their faces, Thomas L and Charles were merrily singing, "Hark the Herald Angels Sing." Everyone inside joyfully shouted, "Merry Christmas!"

For hours, they took turns riding in the Christmas sleigh, singing as they glided through the glistening snow-covered fields at the Catts/Crawford farm.

Everyone stayed at the farm on that special Christmas Eve night. When the children were tucked warmly in featherbeds on the floor, Frances snuggled

44

down among them to read the children's story, "Twas the Night Before Christmas."

This was a Christmas no one would ever forget.

MAMMA'S CRUSTY APPLE DUMPLINGS

Mix:
2 Cups Flour
1 tsp salt
2 Tsp baking powder
½ Cup sweet milk
1 stick Oleo (butter) softened
Roll into a triangle.
Peel and chop 4 large apples
Add ½ Cup sugar and mix well
Pour on rolled out triangle dough. Dot with Oleo (butter)
Roll like a jelly roll. Slice in 1-inch slices. Place slices in a large baking dish.
Syrup:
2 Cups sugar
2 Cups water
1 stick Oleo (butter)
1/4tsp nutmeg
½ tsp cinnamon
Simmer until sugar melts. Pour over apple rolls.
Bake at 350 degrees for about 45 minutes or until golden brown.
Serve with homemade vanilla ice cream with just a hint of cinnamon.

CHAPTER 11

February 1, 1852

I have retreated to our bedroom to escape the noise. We are approaching two months of enjoying George's family living with us. Our seven children, although older, added with their eight; causes me to consider running away from home, at least for a day. I am continually calling the children the wrong name. Perhaps if I write them down, I can keep them straight. Helen Frances, John T.M., Joel, Charles H., Mary, Jane Ann, and Robert belong to us.

Alicia, Jane Ann, Campbell, William, Lucy Cora Bell, Thomas, and Clarence belong to Mary Ann and George. And then there is Fannie who stayed in Virginia to finish school.

Mary Ann wants to help me, but I insist she take care of baby Clarence who is still tiny and frail. George calls Clarence, "Mary's little lamb."

I feel the unending chore of cooking and cleaning has made me exhausted. The extreme cold, snowy weather has kept the kids inside. When Robert is not in court, he and George are at the mercantile near the courthouse, which he will open soon.

Perhaps not the best time to attempt the impossible, I baked a five-layer, chocolate buttermilk cake with white syrup icing. One layer is for each person's birthday. Today is baby Clarence and Mary Ann's birthday. Mama's birthday is February eighth, George's February thirteenth, and Charles will be twenty-one on February fourteenth— Valentine's Day.

Today is also George and Mary Ann's thirteenth wedding anniversary. Soon, we shall leave to go to the farm for a giant celebration supper with Mama. She suggested we set the enormous cake on the birds-eye maple round table that once belonged to her parents. Mama brought the table in the wagon when she and Papa moved to Missouri. Tonight, she will give it to George and Mary Ann as an anniversary gift for their new house.

Before leaving Virginia, Papa asked that his father's silver pocket watch be given to Charles on his twenty-first birthday. Charles asked Mama to wrap up his silver baby spoon with the initials, "C C" to give baby Clarence for his birthday.

I am thankful we are together as a family. I pray God will forgive me for complaining in my moment of weakness or perhaps tiredness.

"I, Jane Ann, can do all things through Christ which strengtheneth me" (Philippians 4:13).

"Wow, all those kids in one house?" Lydia asked. "Where did they all sleep and how long did they have to stand in line for the bathroom?

Looking at Grams, Pops laughed. "I'll let you answer her questions."

Frances and Jane Ann were thankful to have their family together to celebrate birthdays after so many years apart. After everyone arrived, she asked them to circle around the birthday cake Jane Ann made. As planned, she had it sitting on the birds-eye maple table.

Frances asked the family to bow their heads as she prayed. Perhaps, touched that they were all together, Frances called out each family member's name, asking God to bless each one in a special way.

Robert stood on one side of the cake and George on the other. Frances's prayer continued on and on. With his eyes half open Robert noticed the top three layers of the cake had started to slide toward him. He reached over and pushed it back.

George, with one eye open noticed the cake sliding his way. He pushed it back toward Robert. When the prayer ended, the two brothers' hands were covered in white icing, bracing the enormous cake.

Perhaps with so many people in the house and the heat from the fireplace and woodstove, the cake icing had started to melt.

Pops laughed out loud at the thought of two men covered in cake icing.

"It is your turn to read," Grams said as she handed the diary to him.

Pops laughed and said, "Oh no, you forgot to answer Lydia's question. Tell her where the kids slept and how they waited in line for the bathroom."

Well Lydia, back in those days no one had running water or electricity in their house." Grams began telling her. "Big families usually had boys sleep in one room and girls in another. No one had a bed of their own. In fact, they were happy if they had enough room on the bed to sleep without falling off."

Grams wrinkled her nose and said, "For a bathroom, they used an outhouse. Just as sounds, it was outside the house. On cold days, the boys didn't want to wait their turn so they went to the woods. Girls wanted privacy so they waited their turn for the outhouse. Probable with Jane Ann and George's family living together, the girls lined up at the back door to wait their turn, so they wouldn't have to wait in the cold. One would run out of the outhouse, and another would run in. By the time they all took a turn, they probable all had to go again."

Laughing Lydia said, "They must have spent most of their day waiting their turn to go."

Pops took the diary and continued reading.

Spring 1853

Once again, we must say goodbye to Thomas L as he returns to the wagon train. I am not sure how Mama does it. Each time he leaves, she knows in her heart she may never see him again.

I am concerned about little Clarence. Born premature, he has never gained his strength. We all, including the children, pray for him each night. I wonder what will happen in the days ahead.

For now, I will leave my worries with the One who holds the whole world in his hands.

Christmas 1853

Mama wants us to take Christmas dinner to George's house so they will not have to take little Clarence out in the cold. His sweet, innocent smile has touched our hearts. His tiny body must hurt with every move, but yet he is happy.

Just as I learned to fill my name in the Scriptures, I have taught our children to do the same.

"For where your treasure is, Jane Ann, there will your heart be also." (Matthew 6:21)

Our treasure, little Clarence, is in all of our hearts. The best gifts are not something we wrap or give away. They

8013579

are the precious moments when we are with the ones we love, and time hesitates long enough for us to make a memory. Though no one says it, I believe it's on everyone's heart that this might be little Clarence's last Christmas.

As in years past, the family gathered to cut the apple and to read the Christmas story. In silence, they sat by the warm fire, each pondering what the coming days might bring. In a soft, sweet voice, two-year-old little Clarence whispered the words his mama sang to him, "Silent night, holy night."

Joining in, the family sang together.

Jane Ann received a pair of black monogramed gloves for Christmas. Saddened, she knew they would soon be worn to a funeral.

April 16. 1854 Easter Sunday

I ask myself, "How does our heart keep beating when unbearable pain completely takes our breath away? How do we keep breathing when the most painful heartache ever to be imagined, has happened?" I ask God, "What do I do when I hear those I love cry out in pain?" I have always thought that one moment changes life or takes it away forever. As I prayed for God to heal little Clarence, I heard the church bells ring.

Little Clarence died as the church bells rang.

George asked his mother, Frances, if he could bury Clarence at the farm. His grave was the first burial at the Catts/Crawford family cemetery.

"Wasn't there anything the doctor could do to save little Clarence?" Lydia asked.

"At the time they didn't have medicine like we have today," Grams explained. "His life, like all of us, was in God's hands. We don't know how God used the death of little Clarence. But I believe God will never waste someone's pain. He'll use it in a way we may never know or understand. The Catts/Crawford family never recovered from losing little Clarence, but by faith, they accepted it." Grams explained.

Sadly, looking up at Grams, Lydia said, "It must have broken everyone's heart, especially his mama. It hurts me to think of someone so little dying and not being there anymore." She stood and asked if they could take a break.

As she went into the house Grams noticed her eyes were filled with tears. Once inside, she could hear Lydia talking on the phone to her brother, Silas, and her sister Priscilla Rose.

Grams heard Lydia say, "I just wanted to be sure you were both ok."

When Lydia came back out on the porch, Grams thought it best to let Pops read for a while.

Spring 1855

It has been a year since little Clarence passed away. I

refuse to ask God why. As painful as it is, I instead accept God's will.

Thomas L stayed home this spring. Maybe it is because he thinks George will need him, or perhaps he is only tired. He has traveled with the wagon train for ten years. I am still amazed at the stories he shares. I sometimes wonder if he had a lady friend on his last trip west. I will not ask him but instead wait for him to tell me about her.

I am not sure why, but I find myself sitting on our porch staring at nothing while I fall behind in my work. Perhaps little Clarence's death has affected us more than we realize. I need a change. Mama said she is struggling too.

Jane Ann and Frances planned a family picnic day at the farm to celebrate spring. George found someone to watch the mercantile so he could be with his family. The first activity of the day was to play a game called, "Don't touch the ground."

The game was to start on the front porch when everyone arrived. The rules allowed each person to hop, jump, or climb from place to place, but their feet couldn't touch the ground. If someone's feet touched the ground, that person had to start over. Frances had strategically placed boards, empty barrels, and other items as roadblocks to start their game. The first person to reach the blue ribbon tied to the barn door was the winner.

Adults and children had the best time and laughed as they tried to make their way to the barn door without touching the ground. They kept falling and would have to start over.

After a while, Charles got the idea to carry the little ones from place to place, insisting their feet did not touch the ground. Not to be outdone, Thomas L found empty tin cans, often called "air tights," from the barn for the some of the kids to step on and slide their feet across the ground. He also insisted their feet did not touch the ground. To top his brothers, George grabbed feed sacks from the barn and tied them around the rest of the kid's feet. They jumped all the way to the barn. Laughing loudly in fun, George argued that their feet did not touch the ground.

Robert, acting as judge and jury, declared all the children were winners.

Jane Ann, Mary Ann, and Frances brought out the family prize for everyone to enjoy—homemade vanilla ice cream with fresh strawberries.

"I want to play that game with you, Pops," Lydia said, laughing. "I know I can beat you."

"You think so?" Pops replied. "Well, when the rain stops, we'll give it a try. And when your family comes back for you, we'll see if you can beat your brother and sister too."

"We can make it a celebration day," Grams added. "I'll make homemade ice cream like Jane Ann and Frances made as the grand prize."

Lydia nodded. "Yeah, and I'll help crank the ice cream."

Several of the town leaders had taken a liking to George. He was honest, trustworthy, and a fine upstanding citizen in Lawrence County. They wanted him to run for the office of County Treasurer. Hesitant at first, he finally agreed to run for office the following year.

Election Day 1856

I think Papa Catts and Papa Crawford would pop the buttons off their shirts if they were here today. They would be so proud of George. He won the election at nearly 100%. Grouchy old Mr. Weaver voted against George just to be ornery.

Mama and I have a celebration dinner planned at the farm for George. I hope Charles will enjoy the festivities instead of constantly talking about taking a herd of cattle west next spring. This is George's day to celebrate.

Frances and Jane Ann cooked enough food for the entire county. The centerpiece for the table was a sign Thomas L carved for his brother. It read, "George Neal Catts, County Treasurer Lawrence County Missouri."

Those who encouraged George to run for office came to the celebration. They thought he should consider running for mayor in the next election.

Later that evening, George and Mary Ann showed Frances a letter they received from their oldest daughter, Fannie. She'd soon finish school at the Women's Academy of Wellsburg. She wrote, "I will be on my way to Missouri after graduation."

The evening had a festive, happy feeling. Everyone filled their plates and hurried outside to watch the rising of the full pink moon, named after the pink phlox flowers of spring.

Early spring 1857

Robert has tried to talk Charles out of it, but he feels he might as well be talking to himself. Charles is determined and will not listen to anyone. He declares his plans are final. His plan is to leave April 17 from Sedalia, Missouri, to drive one-thousand head of cattle west to northern California.

Thomas L tried to reason with him, explaining how difficult the trail to California is, even without the responsibility of a thousand head of cattle. Trying to help the situation, George offered to sell Charles half of the mercantile if he would change his mind. His answer was firmly, "No."

We all can see Mama is most upset at the thought of him leaving. She has asked God to give her peace if he is to go.

I too am upset Charles is leaving. His dream to take a thousand head of cattle to California is hard for me to imagine. I still think of him as my little brother instead of the man he has become. I realize he has to follow his heart. I will pray for God to give him wisdom to make good decisions and as difficult as it will be, I will leave him in God's care. I'll miss him so much.

Knowing firsthand the difficult trail ahead of Charles and barely having survived many dangerous situations, Thomas L insisted Charles let Robert draw up a will before leaving home.

Charles agreed.

The evening before he was to leave; the Catts/Crawford family circled around him and prayed for God's protection.

Before leaving to go home, Robert advised Charles, "Follow the voice in your heart. The small, still voice in the middle of the night will be God leading you."

The morning Charles left, Frances and Thomas L walked beside his horse to the end of the road.

Frances hugged her son once more then watched as he rode away in a cloud of dust.

Charles left Mount Vernon and headed for Sedalia with a Bible and a letter his Mama secretly slipped in his saddlebag. Thomas L let him borrow Uncle John Neal's silver compass to be sure he found his way back home.

Seeing tears fill his Mama's eyes, Thomas L suggested they walk to her most favorite place in the woods. They both needed to lay their worries at the cross.

Spring 1858

Good news arrived by telegram this morning. Fannie Catts, George and Mary Ann's oldest daughter, will arrive on the afternoon Butterfield Overland Stage. Our family scrambled to get to the depot to meet her. The stage arrived on time with Fannie on board. Since she stayed behind in Virginia to attend the Women's Academy, none of us had ever met her.

George and Mary Ann had not seen her in six years. The children made a sign to welcome Fannie to Mount Vernon.

As we wait for the stage to arrive, I think of the many funny stories I have heard about my niece, Fannie. Mary Ann assures me she is a lovely young girl who seems to just happen into funny situations. She hopes the Women's Academy in Wellsburg has been successful in molding her into a gracious young woman.

With much anticipation, our family watched as the galloping team of horses pulled the Butterfield Overland Stage into town. The Catts/Crawford children held their sign high into the air and cheered as she passed by. She leaned out the window waving with excitement to us all.

We watched as she prepared to make an impressive presentation of her arrival. Tall, beautiful Fannie Catts stood to gracefully step down from the stagecoach. As she leaned out the stage door, the afternoon breeze caught her huge pink hat and blew it a block away. She caught her sleeve on the door and ripped it completely off. As she attempted to step down, we watched as she caught her shoe on the step, losing her balance she fell face down in the dirt. Her pretty pink dress, her pink lace gloves and her face were covered in dirt.

Everyone was shocked as we saw her spring to her feet and sputtered, "I'm okay."

With her unique style, Ms. Fannie Catts had arrived.

For two weeks exhausted Fannie had traveled a grueling twelve-hundred miles by train, riverboat and stage coach to join her family in Missouri. Eighteen year old Fannie came filled with dreams and ambitions to become a school teacher in Mount Vernon.

Summer 1858

Mama is fascinated with Fannie. She makes her laugh trying to be a sophisticated lady in the small town of Mount Vernon. Gracefulness is not one of her attributes. If she is not falling, she is tripping or dropping something. Conversation seems to be difficult for her. She says more things wrong than right.

Grouchy old Mr. Weaver insists, "Ms. Fannie sticks her foot in her mouth more than she stands on it."

When I watch her awkwardly move around, I wonder if she received poor marks in her classes for pose and elegance. Since she and Mama seem to be compatible, and while Charles is away, Mary Ann and George have agreed to let her move to the farmhouse. Perhaps Mama can teach her to be graceful.

One dry, hot afternoon. Frances and Fannie were sitting on the porch waiting for Thomas L to return from town with supplies. A cloud of dust to the west caught their attention. The Butterfield stage was headed into town.

Swatting flies and fanning with an old newspaper, Frances said to Fannie, "I hope Thomas L will check to see if we have any mail on the stage."

Within the hour they could see Thomas L coming up the road with a wagon full of supplies. He pulled the wagon up close to the house so he could unload the house items on the porch.

He pitched a letter to his Mama and said, "It's from Daniel Fulbright. And there is a bag he sent with it."

Thinking it was odd to receive a letter from Dan, Frances handed the letter to Fannie and asked her to read it to her.

Opening the smudged, yellowed envelope, she started reading, "Dear Mrs. Crawford, it is with my deepest sorrow I must tell you that Charles died on May twenty-first."

Closing her eyes, Frances dropped her head to her chest and said to Fannie, "Please go on."

With every word, another tear rolled down Frances's face.

"Charles had been hit in the leg by an Indian arrow. It broke off, causing blood poisoning." Fannie continued, "You would have been proud of him, Mrs. Crawford. While in great pain, he asked the men to get his Bible from his saddle bag and read Scriptures over him until he died ..."

Fannie paused for a moment when she realized Frances was sobbing deeply.

In the letter, Charles asked Daniel to tell his Mama he loved her and to be sure the silver compass was returned to Thomas L. As his last words, Charles said the Lord's Prayer with the men. He then peacefully closed his eyes.

With her apron, Frances wiped her tears away. Without a word, she stood and walked into the house.

Fannie heard the bedroom door close, and through the open window she could hear her grandmother cry.

Leaving the supplies in the wagon, Thomas L turned and walked toward the south woods to be alone.

It seemed life had been sucked out of the family by the death of Charles. Jane Ann, Robert, and George struggled with their grief.

Fannie thought Frances and Thomas L would never get past Charles's death.

Months later, with a grieving heart, Robert executed Charles's will. He left everything to his mother.

Since Charles was buried in California, there would not be a headstone placed in the family cemetery for him. Wanting to do something in memory of his younger brother, Thomas L *carved a sign to hang on the gate.*

Charles H. Crawford
Beloved son of Thomas and Frances Crawford
Born 1831 Wellsburg, Virginia
Died May 21, 1858, Honey Lake, California

CHAPTER 12

July 1859

I pray for Mama. The old enemy of depression is once again rearing its ugly head at her. I know her unshakable faith in God will help her. Perhaps, it is the stress I also feel that is once again making my reading difficult. It seems even the Scriptures are no longer clear. Fannie has kindly offered to help me while she waits to see if a job is available for her to teach school.

Robert had George order a new invention for me called a sewing machine. With it I am making clothes for the family much faster. Friends have asked me to do specialty sewing for them too.

When I go to the mercantile to buy fabric, all I hear is talk of war. It scares me to know war is on the minds of so many. Our family stands firmly with the Union. But Robert has not forgotten what his Uncle Charles taught him about States' Rights. I pray God will be with us in the coming days.

With so much work to be done at the farm to help Mama, I find little if any time to write in my diary. Perhaps that is best for now.

Only God knows the future and the plans he has for each person as well as for the United States. There seemed to be a fog of sadness over the country. No one wanted war, but the reality of war coming meant everyone would be forced to choose a side. Neighbors who've have known one another since they came to homestead the land now pass one another in town and don't speak to each other. The fear of war went deep into the soul of each person. Sadly, their fear was justified. War was coming.

November 6, 1860

Many people stood in line to vote for Mr. Lincoln, praying he will stop war in America before it begins. He is a wise, Godly man who I believe is chosen by God for such a time as this.

How refreshing to hear good news. A young man has stolen the heart of sweet Fannie. They plan to be married next summer. Mama and I are crocheting lace for her wedding dress.

Families prayed for God to guide the nation into the path of peace. And they prayed for President Lincoln as he carried the heavy burden of keeping America as one nation under God. Many sought the peace only God could give to comfort their anxious feeling of eminent war. The reality was that one heart at a time must bow before God to seek peace.

Fannie's upcoming wedding gave the Catts/ Crawford family a break from the fretfulness of war. The excitement of young love gave a refreshing hope that life might one day go back to normal.

Early spring 1861

My heart screams, "Please stop before it is too late." We are not enemies against each other. How can we forget who we are as one nation under God? Has hate filled so many hearts that we are unable to love beyond our differences? Hate is against God. Have we gone so far from God that we are willing to destroy ourselves from within?

I scream, "No," to every shot that will be fired if we go to war. We cannot coldly turn against one another. I don't recognize who we are anymore.

Robert Crawford warned, "If war is declared, it will be the worst decision in America's history."

"In your hands, my dissatisfied fellow-countrymen, and not in mine, is the momentous issue of civil war," Abraham Lincoln proclaimed days before the war started.

The first shots were fired on April 12, 1861.

America was at war. There was no going back, and the worst was yet to come. So many lives were given in the name of who's right and who's wrong. Two selfish hearts would never win. They would both loose more than they could ever imagine. The country had turned against God and had forgotten how to love one another.

Missouri was the only state to officially vote to remain in the Union. Robert Crawford was elected to represent Lawrence County at the Constitutional Convention in Jefferson City, Missouri. Robert Crawford voted for Missouri to remain in the Union.

However, he was most outspoken in his support for States' Rights.

During a confrontation in Saint Louis between the Union and the Missouri Cavalry, many people were injured or killed. Since Missouri was legally part of the Union, Robert adamantly believed during this altercation, the Union attacked their own people.

From this point forward, as a lawyer believing in the rights of each state, he denounced the Union and served with the Missouri Cavalry. Because of his opposition to slavery, he never pledged his allegiance to the Confederacy.

Francis Scott Key, beloved friend of Frances Catts/ Crawford, served on the board of the American Bible Society until his death in 1843. He insisted soldier's Bibles be published and given to every soldier who served America. Robert was one of the soldiers who received a Bible.

"In regard to this great Book, the Bible, I have but to say it is the best gift God has given to man. All the good the Savior gave to the world was communicated through this Book. But for it, we could not know right from wrong. All things most desirable for Man's welfare, here and hereafter, are found portrayed in it." Abraham Lincoln.

Robert wrote his mother a letter to explain his heart change about the war.

After reading his letter, Frances declared she would no longer voice her opinion on the war but instead support all of her sons.

"I don't understand why Frances wouldn't give her opinion anymore," Lydia said.

"The reason was she didn't want any of her sons to think she supported one more than the other. Grams explained. "Until then, the entire family was on the same side. Because of his personal belief, Robert chose to join the opposite side from the family. His decision could possibly put George and Robert as enemies on the battlefield in the war. Rather be a divider between her sons, she instead chose to be a peacemaker by remaining silent in her feelings about the war. The amazing thing about the Catts/Crawford family is their unconditional love. Even war wouldn't break their bond of love."

"Oh, I understand now. She didn't want her sons to think she supported one more than the other." Lydia said.

"That's correct," Pops said. That's what war does; it divides. Frances was wise to not voice her opinion after Robert changed sides. Her love for her family was deeper that the tragedy of war."

"Ready for me to read some more?"

"Yep!"

August 10, 1861

This day I will never forget. My Robert was already gone to serve in the Missouri Cavalry. I couldn't sleep, so I arose early. I finished washing clothes and was hanging them on the lines when I heard a young boy on horseback ride through town, yelling, "Soldiers are in the corn fields above Wilson Creek! Soldiers are a marching from Springfield! A battle is a fixin' to start!"

I hurried to the front of the house where I saw people running every which direction. My heart pounded when I saw my brother George on horseback, galloping past me. I waved, but he never saw me. Our sons, John T. M. and Joel were saddling their horses to join their father. Our family agreed if war broke out, Thomas L would stay to take care of Mama and the rest of the family. He thought that was his way of serving.

I went in the house to be sure everyone was safe. The screen door slammed as I stepped inside. It sounded like a gun shot. That sound echoed in my mind over and over again. I knew the sound meant death to unknown numbers of young men or perhaps even my own sons.

With my family at my side, I rushed to check on Mary Ann. She was sitting on the porch crying. Her children were gathered around her like little chicks around their mother hen. She raised her head to look at me, and I could see the fear in her tear-filled eyes.

Sadly, we knew our husbands might meet as enemies on the battlefield. Crying, Mary Ann said, "God help us all."

Sobbing, I reached for her hand and whispered, "Our Father, which art in heaven, Hallowed be Thy name. Thy kingdom come, Thy will be done ..." She joined in as our voices became louder. We kept repeating, "Thy will be done. Thy will be done."

The only thing the Catts/Crawford family could pray was for God's will to be done.

Robert was Frances's stepson, Jane Ann's husband, and George and Thomas L's stepbrother.

George was Frances's son, Mary Ann's husband, and Jane Ann and Thomas L's brother.

Robert and George had been close brothers since the day their parents married.

As soon as Frances heard the news of the battle, she went to her room and fell to her knees.

Fannie's fiancé rode by the farm to let her know he was leaving for the Wilson Creek battle.

All anyone could do was to trust those they loved to God's hands and to continue praying for God's will to be done.

Thomas L had dug a cellar at the edge of the woods months before. He planned it as a place for the women and children to hide. He ran to the woods to check supplies which he laid up weeks before. He covered the cellar with brush when he left.

Running back to the house, he made sure his mother and Fannie were alright. He hurried to hitch the horses to the wagon and headed into town. Once he arrived, he loaded the Catts and Crawford families along with Jane Ann and Mary Ann into the wagon.

Before he rode off to Wilson Creek, George gathered the cash from the mercantile and took it home to Mary Ann. He then rushed to the courthouse for the county's money. To protect the county's funds from thieves, he buried the money but didn't tell anyone where he hid it. He said goodbye to his family and rode away, yelling over his shoulder to Mary Ann for her to set a plate for him for supper.

They headed back to the farm where Thomas L could protect them if needed.

Jane Ann and Mary Ann were right; Robert and George did meet on the battlefield.

George was hit by shrapnel not long after he entered the battle.

Robert, serving with the Missouri Cavalry, charged up a hill when his horse was shot, throwing Robert to the ground. When he tried to stand up, he was hit in the chest with a bullet. He fell backward on the ground. Rubbing his chest, he realized the Soldier's Bible in his shirt pocket stopped the bullet.

Robert heard someone nearby moaning, and a familiar voice calling, "Help me, please help me."

His brother George.

Robert crawled over to him, pulled him from the battlefield, and flagged down a passing medical wagon going to the makeshift hospital.

Robert held George's hand to help him up onto the wagon. Still holding on as the wagon pulled away, George said, "Blood brothers forever."

That was the last time Robert saw his beloved brother.

The Battle of Wilson Creek lasted less than six hours. Bodies of dead and injured soldiers were left to lie in the hot August sun all over the fields. Many of the men who fought in the battle didn't have uniforms. No one even knew which side they fought for.

War divided the nation. Divided meant everyone had to choose a side. Fathers were against their sons, brothers were against brothers, and families who loved one another fought against each other.

Frances Catts/Crawford refused to allow the war to divide her family. She was the prayer soldier that fought with all of her heart to keep her family together.

She remembered The House Divided speech given by Abraham Lincoln on June 16, 1858 when he said, "A house divided against itself cannot stand." He based it on Mark 3:25 in the Bible.

George made it to a hospital in Springfield. There he died not of his battle wounds but of typhoid fever. His attending doctor made sure his body was returned to the family for burial. George was buried next to his son, little Clarence, in the family cemetery.

Under the grove of oak trees which surrounded the cemetery, the Catts children cried for their father. The rest of the family and community wept with them. Hidden in the woods, fearful he would be caught by enemy soldiers, Robert watched his brother's funeral from a distance.

After the funeral, Mary Ann, Jane Ann, Thomas L, and Frances walked to the cross in the forest. They joined hands and circled the cross to pray. Robert quietly stepped out from behind a tree and took the hands of Jane Ann and his mother, Frances. As quickly and silently as he came, he left.

Uncaring about Mary Ann's grief painful of losing her husband, some of the town's people questioned her about where the county's money was hidden. Some even said she kept the money. Their hurtful harassment made losing George even more painful.

The black gloves Jane Ann wore to the funeral, she folded to put away and prayed she would never have to wear them again.

Christmas 1861

I refuse to let worry overcome me. I remind myself, worry is the worthless conversation I have with myself. Prayer is the powerful conversation I have with God. To my knees I fall both morning and night. My faith fills me with hope.

It does not seem like Christmas. All of our hearts are heavy, and Christmas is the last thing on my mind. I remind myself Christmas is not about us but instead the birth of our Savior. The reality is Robert and my sons are away at war, George has died, and America is shattered. I must stay strong so I can care for our family. Mama and Mary Ann need me. I am thankful Thomas L is with us. Still saddened, I have not heard from Robert or our sons in months.

I know we are being watched, so I must be careful. I will no longer write about the war in my diary. If taken from me, I do not want anything I write to bring harm to Robert.

I am encouraged by the words of Victor Hugo in one of my favorite books, "Les Miserable," written by Charles E. Wilbur.

"Certain thoughts are prayers. These are moments when, whatever be the attitude of the body, the soul is on its knees."

I feel ashamed I have not thought about the children's Christmas. They need to be protected as the last innocence of war. I will dry my eyes, tie on my apron, and help Mama make Sweet Milk Sugar Cookies for Christmas morning. I will sew all night if needed to make gifts for those I love. My treasured silver thimble will once again be used to bring joy to others.

I am thankful God has opened my heart to the hope only Christmas can bring. I am determined to gasp a deep breath of hope and remind myself, hope is forever.

Since Thomas L was the only man at home, he sliced the apple to tell the story about the Bethlehem Star. He asked Jane Ann to read the Christmas story from the family Bible.

Jane Ann was hesitant to read out loud and afraid she would stumble on the words like she did as a child. Accepting the Bible into her hands, she cleared her throat and began to read. "And it came to pass..." Tired and nervous, she stumbled on some of the words. The children gathered close and helped her.

"Your Mom use to help me with my reading, Lydia," Grams interrupted. "When she was learning to read, she would sit on the counter in the kitchen while I was cooking supper and read to me. She would sound out the words she was learning in school, and I would sound them out with her. We learned together. She did the same for her sister, your Aunt Cassi. They would sit on the porch swing and read together.

"I struggled with reading, but there wasn't a name for it when I was growing up. Your Aunt Cassi's teacher recognized she had a problem, but very little was done to help her. Aunt Cassi learned to deal with her dyslexia on her own, just as I did."

"I didn't know Aunt Cassi was dyslexic too. She's so creative and is so much fun. I had no idea." Lydia said.

"I have Mom's help, a tutor, and teachers who understand how to help me. And I know what my problem is. It is called dyslexia." Lydia added. "Please, may I read now?" She looked at Pops and said with a smile, "If Grams and Aunt Cassi can learn to live with being dyslexic, so can I."

The following spring, knowing the men were away, bushwhackers with ill intentions visited the farm. Shamed and humiliated, they learned a hard lesson—do not mess with the Catts/Crawford family.

Christmas 1863

It is hard to believe it is Christmas time again. It is even harder to believe the war continues, and Robert is not home. I pray our boys are safe as they serve with their father. He leads his soldiers with God as his Commander in Chief.

Young soldiers from both sides often stop by the farm begging for food. Many are on their way home. I don't care which side they serve on, I see the eyes of my own sons.

I pray someone is there for them when they are in need.

I still often think about the story Mama told us about Papa Catts and his soldiers during the War of 1812. When they were in need, nearby families gave all they had and did without themselves. I pray I will do the same for the soldiers.

I thank God for whoever is helping my sons and Robert. I keep a pot of soup on the stove or on the fire outside. Sometimes I have to boil chicken bones over and over again for broth. Whatever we have, we share with the soldiers. I can't imagine ever turning away anyone who is hungry, no matter how little we have.

Mama, Mary Ann, and I have decided we will make the best of what we have for Christmas. I tore scrap fabric into strips for the children to make angel rag dolls. Mary Ann found buttons and string for them to make button spinners. Fannie brought paper, pencils, and scissors to make paper dolls and paper bears. Mama has saved sugar and honey for months to have enough to make the Sweet Milk Sugar Cookies. They will be small, but everyone will receive one.

While we gathered around the kitchen table making Christmas toys, we heard singing. I opened the door and there stood, our neighbors, the Thrasher family, covered in snow, singing, "Silent Night, Holy Night." We invited them inside to warm by the fire.

Hidden under her coat, Mrs. Thrasher had a gift. She said, "All we have to bring you is a small basket of apples."

We asked them to please stay and have Christmas dinner with us. Their children and our children made gifts for each other from the rags and buttons. Our house was filled with love.

After we finished eating, Thomas L asked us to gather around the fire because he had a story he wanted to tell us. I handed him the basket of apples. After he finished the story, he sliced more apples and handed each child a piece so they could nibble the apple around the star. He then asked Mr. Thrasher if he would read the Christmas story from our family Bible.

As I looked around the room, my heart filled with gratitude to God. The sound of laughter and seeing the children smile made me realized this was my Christmas gift from God. My heavy heart filled with joy as I counted the blessings that surrounded me.

As we sat around the warm fire, I asked God to bring a special blessing to Robert and our sons and to bring them safely home.

After an unexpected and amazing Christmas, Thomas L offered to take the Thrasher family home in the sleigh. They loaded up quickly and were ready to go when Mama hurried out to return Mrs. Thrasher's basket filled with Sweet Milk Sugar Cookies.

Mr. and Mrs. Thrasher had no idea what a treasured gift they had brought for our family.

If only for one night—Christmas eve—war didn't exist. Only God's love.

Days before Christmas, some shameful deserters of the war came through Lawrence County, raiding people's barns and cellars. A no-good group attempted to steal from the Catts/Crawford's cellar, but Thomas L ran them off with a shot gun.

From the Thrasher family, they stole everything from their cellar except a small basket of apples. God saved the apples so the children could hear the story of the Bethlehem Star.

Since several inches of snow covered the ground, Thomas L wanted to surprise everyone with a sleigh ride. He whispered to Jane Ann that he needed help in the barn. Once in the barn, he and Jane Ann hurried to harness the horse to the sleigh. As he secured the last buckle, he turned to her and said, "Your Christmas surprise is standing behind you."

When Jane Ann turned around, she saw Robert standing in front of her. She melted into his arms.

Robert had sent a message to Thomas L saying, "I will be in the barn at nine o'clock on Christmas Eve. Please, let it be my Christmas surprise for Jane Ann."

October 31, 1864

Thomas L heard a group of bushwhackers were burning farms in the area. On the darkest night, we stood in shock on our front porch. We watched the blazing fires and black smoke roaring above our neighbor's farm. Thomas L thought we should get prepared to face the worst.

Mama had a plan to save as much as we could if they hit our farm. Most of the food was hidden in the secret root cellar in the woods. Quilts and furniture were stacked on the back porch, ready to carry away from the house. Cast iron pots and items from the kitchen were upside down in the field behind the house. Thomas L built cages for the chickens and turkeys. We hurried to carry them to the edge of the woods and decided we would rather the coyotes get them than the bushwhackers.

Our cherished Christmas sleigh was already hidden deep in the woods. We quickly took the horses to the backside of the woods. Thomas L heaped hay on the wagon. and we pushed it into the woods south of the barn.

His guns loaded, Thomas L will only use them if his hand is called.

Mama placed the sign from the mantel and the box containing the piece of the flag in a crate by the back door. She picked up the box containing the family Bible and held it close to her heart for just a moment before laying it on top of the crate. We have done all we can to save as much as we can. Please God, protect us from the evil we know is coming. I will hide my diary and what little cash money we have in the secret pocket I sewed under my dress.

The evil did come with flaming torches held high. The cowards had their shameful faces covered as if God himself couldn't see them. In shock, the Catts/ Crawford family stood in the rain watching the last smoldering embers burn. Everything was completely burned to the ground.

By evening, Thomas L already had the horses hitched to the wagon and pulled it back near where the house had been. He tugged to pull the canvas bonnet over the wagon and carried a feather mattress up from the cellar along with some quilts.

Frances Catts/Crawford would once again sleep in the covered wagon in which she and Thomas Crawford traveled to Missouri. Thomas L would sleep on the possum belly of the wagon so he could keep an eye out for the bushwhackers. The rest of the family went back to Mary Ann's house in town.

The next morning, neighbors and friends came early, ready to build another one-room cabin.

Spring 1865

I watched the soldiers walking on our road. Many I knew were young when the war started and now look battle worn and old. I am upset to see so many using small tree limbs as crutches. They hobbled step by step, trying to get home to their families. I offer them food as a way to thank them for serving no matter what side they fought on, and I ask to pray with them. Some are angry and refuse my prayers. Others ask me to pray for their family and those they love. Many look at me and begin to cry. I have torn most of our clothes and bedding to use for bandages for the injured. I pray the fever or poison in their body will heal. If only I could help more.

My heart sinks when I begin to question the war. Did we do this horrible thing to ourselves? Did so many have to die for a war that has no winners? Will we ever be able to forgive ourselves or will God ever forgive us? I have so many questions and no answers.

I am thankful Robert and our boys survived the war, but I feel guilty as I help bandage the wounds of other mother's sons.

The country had nothing to celebrate. Instead of joining as one to find an answer to our problems, we instead chose to pour out the blood of our brothers. Blood would remain in the soil of every battlefield forever. Rivers and streams will never wash clean the blood that was spilled in them. All Americans were responsible for every soldier who died. They could only blame themselves.

We should question what we taught our children by our example. The deep wounds of that war would never heal. When people don't love God more than themselves, they will always be at war with one another.

God is the only hope for future generations.

Five days after the war ended, another man was needlessly killed. News of his death spread like wildfire. When soldiers heard the name of who died, many looked into the eyes of their enemy, turned, and walked away. Perhaps at that moment they questioned if they too were responsible for his death.

His death knocked our nation to their knees. One moment changed the heart of a nation. President Abraham Lincoln died on April 15, 1865, by the hand of a coward who never served as a soldier.

America grieved for the man their hate had killed. Perhaps it was his death that turned America toward repentance so healing could begin.

Some thought if President Lincoln were asked if his life were more important than any other soldier on either side, he would humbly reply no.

"If my people which are called by My name, shall humble themselves, and pray and seek my face, and turn from their wicked ways; then will I hear from heaven, and will forgive their sin, and will heal their land" (II Chronicles 7:14).

Only with God could a broken nation be healed.

After President Lincoln was killed, people wanted

to know more about the man who held our nation together to the end of the war. He was a man of great stature, six foot, four inches tall.

With his famous stovetop hat, he appeared to be seven feet tall. People looked up to him as our leader during the worst war in American history.

Some said he wore the stovetop hat for a specific purpose. He used it to store important documents and maps. He hid the papers in the lining or inside rim of his hat.

Many people didn't know Edwin Booth, brother of Lincoln's assassin, John Wilks Booth, saved the life of President Lincoln's son, Robert Todd Lincoln. While young Robert stood on a train platform in Jersey City, New Jersey, curious passengers came uncomfortably close to him. He stepped backward and fell into the space between the platform and a moving train. The hand that reached down to grab him by his coat collar to safety was that of Edwin Booth. Robert recognized him as the famous stage actor.

The day Edwin Booth was buried, June 9, 1893; Ford's Theater collapsed and killed 22 people.

President Lincoln signed legislation to create the Secret Service on April 14, 1865, to combat the growing problem of currency counterfeiters. That was the day before he died. He told his bodyguard he had a dream he would be assassinated.

Years later, the Secret Service was assigned responsibility of guarding the president.

President Lincoln was a man who thought long and hard on decisions he made. With so much on his mind, more times than not, he didn't eat. He especially didn't like big meals. Never liking breakfast, he ate little in the mornings and sometimes only an apple for lunch. His favorite meal was chicken fricassee served with cornmeal rail splitters.

Chicken fricassee was a fancy name given to an old farm recipe. When a hen became too old to lay eggs or a rooster was too old to perform his rooster duties, they were relegated to the stew pot. The old bird was said to create a wise, flavorful dish served with cornmeal sticks baked in a stick pan. Whenever the White House had guests for dinner, Abe Lincoln would ask someone to pass the rail splitters. This nickname for the cornbread sticks was from his first campaign slogan, "Abe Lincoln the Rail Splitter." Lincoln was a poor, self-educated lawyer, who grew up splitting rails to build split-rail fences.

Mr. Lincoln also enjoyed ginger crackers or as some called them, "Lincoln's Gingerbread Men." His favorite, however, was Mrs. Lincoln's famously remembered White Almond Cake.

That afternoon, Pops suggest they stop reading for a while so he could move the cattle. He needed to herd them through the gate into a field of fresh green grass.

"Lydia," Grams said. "How would you like to help me cook Pops an Able Lincoln supper?"

"Yes, that sounds like fun," she answered.

They spent all afternoon cooking Chicken Fricassee, Rail Splitters, Ginger Crackers and White Almond Cake. Grams remembered seeing a black stovetop hat in one of the hat boxes in the attic. She and Lydia searched until they found the hat and had it sitting on Pops' chair when he came in for supper.

"This Abe Lincoln supper was amazing," he said. "Thanks for preparing it for me."

Lydia smiled and gave Pops a hug.

JUST A MOMENT

HONEST ABE'S CORNMEAL RAIL SPLITTERS

1 Cup flour
4 Tsp baking powder
2 eggs
3 Tbs sugar
1 tsp salt
1 Cup yellow corn meal
4 tsp melted shortening
1 Cup buttermilk
1/2 tsp baking soda, dissolved in 1 tsp cold water

Preheat the oven to 375 degrees. Grease/butter a muffin tin or cornbread-stick pan.

In a small bowl, sift together the flour and baking powder. Set aside.

In a large bowl, beat the eggs. Add the sugar, salt, and corn meal. Mix together and add the shortening. Mix again, add the buttermilk, and stir to combine.

Add the baking soda/water mixture to the batter, followed by the flour mixture. Stir until well combined.

Put cornbread-stick pan into oven with ½ tsp of oil in each slot. Heat to the sizzling point and fill about ¾ full.

Bake until lightly browned, about 12 minutes. Serve hot with honey butter.

CHAPTER 13

Summer 1865

Robert and our family returned home from Texas where he had been assigned to soldier recruitment in the year 1864. We would not have been together had it not been for Thomas L. He risked his life to take our family to the boarder of Arkansas and Texas to meet Robert.

Life was difficult in Texas. The long, devastating years of war seemed to suck the life out of Robert. His strong spirit is weak, and he is tired.

I look at him now, and he is not only broken physically but also financially. Before the war, we saved every penny we could to buy land. We helped others buy land and settle in Lawrence and Greene County. Everything was taken from us except our house in Mount Vernon. We thank God everyday Robert is alive and can work as a lawyer once again.

Tomorrow, I will go with Robert to Springfield where he will meet Mr. Anderson who is coming in from Memphis on the Butterfield Overland Stage at noon. He has a large cattle farm on the Strawberry River in Arkansas.

We will stay in town and pick up special items Mary Ann needs for the mercantile. There is still much tension in Springfield from the war.

Jane Ann and Robert traveled to Springfield early Friday morning on July 21st. As soon as they arrived in town, they checked their buggy and horse at Mr. Burk's stable. They hoped to rent a room above Smith's Tavern, a stop for the Butterfield Overland Stage Line, located on Booneville, just north of the town square. This was considered the best place to meet Mr. Anderson.

Thinking perhaps they would need a cross breeze on a hot July night, Robert requested a corner room with a window on each side. While he was signing the hotel registry, the desk clerk warned Robert there might be trouble in town that night.

Jane Ann stayed in their room while Robert met with Mr. Anderson in the Tavern lobby. From the big windows in their room, she noticed groups of men gathering to talk. One man seemed to be going from group to group, showing the men a watch. Intrigued, Jane Ann kept an eye on what was happening on the street until Robert finished his meeting.

Around five-o'clock, Robert went to get Jane Ann so they could go for an early supper. They returned to their room just before six p.m..

The infamous gunfighter, James Butler Hickok, better known as Wild Bill Hickok, had been in a poker game the night before with Davis Tutt. He lost several games and owed Tutt a good amount of money. They bickered about payment. Hickok agreed to let Tutt keep his Waltham repeater gold watch until he could pay him the next day. To not embarrass Hickok, Tutt had to agree not to show the watch in public.

But unable to resist, Tutt showed his friends the watch the next day. Around six that evening, Hickok became extremely angry when he saw Tutt on the street wearing his watch.

Hickok calmly turned toward Tutt and called out, "Dave, here I am."

Tutt assumed the sideways duelist's stance and reached for his gun. Hickok faced off with him, seventy-five yards apart, with his Navy Colt ivory handled revolver. Drawing his gun, butt-handle forward, Hickok steadied his right wrist with his left hand.

They fired simultaneously.

Tutt missed. Hickok shot straight through Tutt's heart, killing him instantly. As he fell to the street, Tutt said, "Boys, I'm killed."

Hearing lots of commotion and yelling from the street, Jane Ann and Robert watched the gunfight from the big window in their room. They were too far away to see who fired the first shot. Their story of seeing the famous gunfight between Wild Bill Hickok and Davis Tutt was passed down from generation to generation.

This famously became known as the first Wild West gunfight.

Hickok was arrested and tried for manslaughter. He was acquitted by the courts as being a fair fight. Remaining in Springfield after the trial, he later ran for Sherriff. Most people thought he was too hot headed to hold that position and refused to vote for him. A few years later he settled at Deadwood in the Dakota Territory. There, he was shot in the back by "Crooked Nose Jack" McCall.

Known as the fastest gun in the west, Wild Bill Hickok died at the age of thirty-nine.

Christmas 1865

In some ways, I feel guilty but also forever grateful that Robert and our sons survived the war. We are together for Christmas. It has been four years since our beloved George died. Mary Ann is still so lonely.

My bittersweet feelings will never go away. My husband lived. Mary Ann's husband, my brother, died. I can only trust in knowing God chooses who will live and who will die. Robert and I do all we can for Mary Ann's family. Perhaps, this is the reality of life we have to live with. I must empty my heart in prayer and ask God to bless us with a good Christmas.

Jane Ann and Robert were welcomed home to Mount Vernon after the war. Robert was like most soldiers who survived—flat broke and in poor health.

The Catts/Crawford family was nothing less than amazed at how they loved and supported one another. The war that divided a nation didn't divide their family. If anything, their love for each other deepened.

When Frances heard Robert was home from the war and coming to see her, she walked to the end of the road to welcome her son home.

Mary Ann and her family welcomed him with open arms. A letter George wrote before he died explained how Robert helped him as a brother on the battlefield.

Thomas L chose to put his life in danger many times to protect his family during the war. He chose to serve his country by staying home to care for all of his family while others went to war.

Jane Ann said her mother often pondered in her heart the things which happened in her life. Robert left for war, George left for a battle, and Charles left to go to California. Thomas L willingly stayed behind to do the work of four men to care for his family. She said each was called according to God's plan.

The first Christmas after the war ended was a soul-searching time for the family. Each person had to decide if they wanted peace, first within their heart, then within their family, and last, as a nation. Peace had to be a decision for each individual.

Frances Catts/Crawford lost two husbands, three sons, and her home and barn which were burned to the ground. She fought and won the battle of bitterness in her life. With her grandchildren listening, she prayed for the bushwhackers who burned her farm, those who accused Mary Ann of stealing the county's money, and for the Indian who shot the arrow that killed Charles. She prayed for those who meant harm to anyone in her family. Frances said, "Let there be peace in our great nation. And let it begin in my heart."

Jane Ann reminded her family, "Blessed are the peacemakers; for they shall be called the children of God."

On Christmas Eve, the family gathered once again around a warm fire but this time with more grateful, forgiving hearts than ever before.

Thomas L stood to tell the story of the Bethlehem Star. He handed Robert the knife and apple and said, "Welcome home."

Spring 1866

We are building a new house and a barn at the farm for Mama. She has never complained about living in the one-room cabin we built after the bushwhackers burned the farm. Robert wants her to have a porch big enough for a swing and rocking chairs. Thomas L has promised he will again build her matching "his and hers" outhouses.

Sadly, Mama's big, sweet-smelling lilac bushes burned along with the house. I dug her starts from my bushes, and I will plant them where the southwest breeze will deliver the beautiful smell of lilac to her bedroom. She told me morning is the time she most thinks of Papa and those she loves.

The house we are building will probably be her last home. She is now seventy-five years old.

I wonder how my children, now that they are grown and are starting families of their own, think of me. I see Mama as the strongest, most compassionate woman I have ever known. I continue to hope I can be like her.

Rebuilding America was under way. So much had been destroyed during the war which had to be replaced. The expansion of the railroad was connecting the country. People were once again extending a hand to neighbors, unconcerned about what side they supported during the war. Perhaps we were once again one nation under God, united as one. The question was, would God ever bless America again?

Summer 1869

Robert wakes up at night sweating and in fear. He has horrible dreams about the war. Sometimes he talks in his sleep. I wonder who the young boy is he keeps telling to go home. He mumbles in his sleep, "You are too young to be a soldier. Go home: go home."

One thing still seems to haunt him about the war—an unfinished task. I am convinced he feels he must do something before he can be at rest.

John Catts's father, Michael Catts, was a Revolutionary War commander. When John Catts was a soldier in the War of 1812, his father wisely advised him to, "Bury your dead soldiers as you go, that is the least they deserve for serving our country."

Knowing John Catts's strong belief in this act of respect, Frances gave Robert the same bit of advice when he joined the Missouri Cavalry.

More than twenty-three hundred soldiers were killed at the Battle of Wilson Creek. An estimated three hundred were killed at the second Battle of Springfield. When the out-of-control wildfire of war raged on, no one had time to bury the dead.

Remembering what Frances told him about burying the dead soldiers, Robert Crawford couldn't stand to think about the ones who were pushed into a ravine, buried in shallow graves, or the many injured men who died alone. He knew they were someone's son, father, brother, or friend.

One night as he stood guard, substituting for the tired men under his command, he thought about how many soldiers had been left behind. That night he promised God if he survived the war, he would go back and bury the dead soldiers.

The National Cemetery in Springfield Missouri was established in 1867 for all soldiers who served America except those who served in the Confederacy. Robert wanted a resting place for all soldiers, no matter what side they served on. In 1867, Robert served on the board of the Confederate Association and began working with the Daughters of the Confederacy to establish the only Confederate Cemetery in Missouri.

Robert completed the legal papers to buy land which adjoined the National Cemetery. Sadly, a rock wall had to be built to separate the two cemeteries.

Shortly after acquiring the land, Robert personally traveled to Wilson Creek and began his search for soldier remains. He and many others personally dug the graves at the new cemetery and properly buried the remains of over five-hundred soldiers. Of those individuals, only four were identified with names.

Some have thought those who buried the soldiers should have also been honored for such selfless deeds. The first Decoration Day for the Confederate Cemetery was June 1870, five years after the war ended.

At that event, Robert Crawford said, "Every person deserves a resting place."

While searching for soldier's remains on Bloody Hill, as it was later called, Robert recognized the place where his brother George had been injured. He walked over to the position where he remembered helping George onto the medical wagon. There, Robert bent down on one knee, his tears falling on the hallowed battleground where so many soldiers died and grieved for his brother George.

Barely able to utter the words, he said, "Blood brothers forever."

Robert W. Crawford was a good man. Right or wrong in what he believed or the side he served during the war, he was a good, compassionate man who loved God.

October 1873

The love of my life is gone. I don't want to live without Robert. We suffered through so many difficult times during the war. Everything was taken from us except our home. Robert pulled himself out of the dark shadow of war to build a new life for our family. With broken-down health, he courageously carried on. He spent his life serving God, caring for our family, and helping others. He loved everyone, even those who hurt him. He is gone, and my heart is broken. I struggled to breathe to think I would have to live without Robert.

One moment has changed my life forever. I remember Mama asking after Papa died, "What will I do without him?" Now I must ask myself, "What will I do without Robert?" I would rather have died with him than to go on without him. However, that is not my choice to make, only God's. My choice is to be thankful for the life we shared.

Highly respected and honored attorney, Robert W. Crawford, collapsed with pneumonia while at court in Nevada Missouri. At age sixty-one, he died peacefully on October 19, 1873, with his wife, Jane Ann, faithfully at his side. He is buried near his brother George at the family cemetery.

After speaking words of comfort to the family, Pastor Gilmore turned to Jane Ann and said, "For where your treasure is, Jane Ann, there your heart will be also."

One moment changes life. Only two days before, the family celebrated Jane Ann's sixtieth birthday. As a birthday gift, Frances gave her the blue broach which had once belonged to her mother. Her father had given it to her as a wedding gift in 1774. Frances let Jane Ann wear the family treasure on her wedding day as something borrowed and something blue. The broach would now belong to Jane Ann.

To celebrate Jane Ann's sixtieth, Thomas L built a bonfire for the kids and played his fiddle so everyone could dance. Robert and Jane Ann stood on the porch with their arms around one another, watching their family enjoy the party. Thomas L called out to his brother to dance with his birthday bride.

Thomas L played a new song, "Silver Threads Among the Gold."

When the song ended, Robert took his birthday gift from his pocket and put it around Jane Ann's neck—a gold, heart-shaped necklace with a cross in the center.

Looking into Jane Ann's eyes Robert said, "It represents what means the most to me, my love for you and the cross of Christ."

Touching the beautiful necklace, Jane Ann responded, "I will wear it forever."

This unforgettable, loving moment lingered in the minds of everyone long after the party.

For weeks before the party, Robert seemed tired and not feeling well. Jane Ann was deeply concerned about him. Knowing he needed to be in Nevada for court on Monday, she insisted she travel with him.

Not having been in court with Robert for many years, Jane Ann sat in the back to watch the proceedings. The cough Robert had battled for days seemed to worsen while he was giving his closing statement to the jury. As he turned to sit down, he collapsed to the floor. Jane Ann rushed to his side. Several men took him to their hotel room where Jane Ann sat beside him in his last moments. Holding on to the heart necklace with the cross, she kissed his cheek and wept.

Picking up his hand and holding it against her heart, she softly asked, "What will I do without you, Robert?"

The next morning Jane Ann traveled back to Mount Vernon with Robert's body. She would once again lay out her black gloves to wear to a funeral. Thomas L built Robert's casket and on top carved a heart with a cross.

When the men who'd served with Robert during the war heard of his passing, out of respect for the family, they came to carry his casket to the cemetery. At the funeral, friends and family who loved and respected Robert Crawford surrounded the Catts/Crawford cemetery.

After the funeral, Robert's close friend, Arthur, told the family, "Robert lived with amazing grace."

After the war ended, Robert held no bitterness but instead showed grace and forgiveness to everyone. He was injured several times. Robert escaped to Oklahoma when a bounty was placed on his head for allowing one of his men to go home for Christmas while his wife delivered their baby. The bounty was removed by his commanding officer, but he continued to be hunted throughout the war by his adversaries.

He never recovered his financial losses. Even when the land he bought twenty-five years before the war was taken from him, he forgave those who took it from his family.

Arthur shared with the family stories Robert told him while his wife, Shirley, stayed with Jane Ann.

The most dangerous experience for Robert was when he was separated from his soldiers after the second battle for Springfield. While trying to find a place to hide along the Findley River, a snake startled his horse. Robert was thrown to the ground, and his horse ran off into the woods. Having to walk a long distance and trying to stay clear from his enemies, he found an old fishing shack near Garrison Springs in which to hide.

Earlier, Robert heard Union soldiers talk about hiding food and supplies near Smallin Cave. Here in a deep pool of spring water, soldiers came to swim and bath, out of sight from their enemies.

Robert's best guess it was a three-mile walk to the cave area. Once rested, he started his journey, hoping he wouldn't encounter many soldiers guarding the cave.

A smaller cave above Smallin Cave was known as "The Cave of the Lost Battalion." Covered with a brushy growth with a small entrance at one side, Robert could see only a few soldiers inside guarding the supplies. He piled dried grass and sticks together a distance from the cave. He set it on fire and threw what little ammunition he had into the fire.

Hurrying, he hid behind a huge rock for protection and waited. The soldiers, sitting around a fire just inside the cave, heard the gun fire. They cautiously ran outside to assess the danger.

Robert wound through the brush covering the entrance and quickly ducked into the cave, grabbed some ammunition before hurrying to the back of the cave. The soldier's campfire gave him just enough dim light to make his way deeper into the cavern where he could hunker down in silence.

Unsure what caused the blasting noise, the soldiers returned to their task of guarding the supplies.

Robert felt hopelessly trapped. He tried to think of a distraction he could create so he could escape. He began hearing scratching sounds from the dark abyss. Recognizing the sound, he took off his cloak and started slinging it around, hitting the walls of the cave. He immediately laid flat on the cave floor and covered his head with his cloak. Suddenly, an overpowering swarm of bats filled the cave, forcibly pushing their way out the entrance.

At the sound of bats coming at them, the soldiers panicked and immediately ran from the cave. This gave Robert enough time to make his way to the front, grab more ammunition and a handful of food, and then dart through the brushy maze to safety.

Soldiers under Robert's command heard the commotions of the enemy soldiers running from the cave and watchfully came to search for him. Robert jumped onto the back of the saddle with one of his soldiers, and they returned safely to camp.

The next day in his report to his commanding officer, Robert listed in detail the supplies and ammunition he saw in the cave.

Arthur's chin began to quiver as he said, "My friend, my leader, Colonel Robert Crawford was known by his commanding officers as a soldier with great courage and bravery, gallantry to his men and honored for a quick mind to make accurate decisions."

Jane Ann added, "His father, Thomas Crawford, would have been proud that he was called a man of great faith by those who knew him best. And that he lived as a good example to others. He never, ever allowed bitterness or hatred to fill his heart after the war. His love was unconditional. He offered grace even if it was never returned to him. I am proud he was my husband, the father of our children and the love of my life."

John Newton said it best, "Amazing grace, how sweet the sound..."

CHAPTER 14

Summer 1876

I am happy for Mama. Fannie and Thomas L are taking her to America's Centennial Celebration in Philadelphia. They will travel by train first to Wellsburg then to Washington D.C., on to Baltimore, and their final stop will be to attend the celebration.

Mama wants to see the piece of woodwork created by Robert's nephew, George B Crawford titled, "The Centennial Memorial Bracket." It was sculpted from seventy-six different kinds of Virginia wood and will be on display in Independence Hall. Our family is honored George's work was selected to be shown during America's Centennial.

They are keeping me busy making new clothes for their trip. Fannie is pleased with the black-and-rose-colored tapestry bag I made for her. I am making Mama a fine, beautiful hat to wear. Thomas L thus far is refusing to wear the black top hat I made for him. They asked me to go with them, but home is where I want to be for now.

Lydia interrupted with excitement, "Maybe the stovetop hat from the attic is the one Thomas L wore to the Centennial."

"Hmm. You're probably right," Pops said.

Grams nodded, then continued Jane Ann's diary entry.

It has been three years since Robert died. Every day I ask God to help me go on with my life without him. I understand now how Mama could not let go of her love for Papa.

I ask God to pour upon me, Jane Ann, the fruits of your Spirit: love, joy, peace, patience, kindness, goodness, faithfulness, gentleness, and self-control from Galatians 5:22-23.

"I know that Scripture, Grams. But why did Jane Ann want God to give her those gifts if the one she loved most was gone?" Lydia asked.

"She wanted to love the family that she still had and live the J-O-Y she learned from her mother," Grams explained. "Lydia, she wanted to experience all the gifts only God could give to make her life worthwhile. She needed a purpose to go on."

"That would be really hard to do," Lydia said.

"Yes, it would be very difficult." Grams agreed. "But God's Word reminds us it is God who gives us strength. Philippians 4:13 says, 'I can do all this through him who gives me strength.'" As humans, we aren't able to do these things by ourselves, but with God's help, we can get through anything."

"I remember how Jane Ann filled her name into God's promises," Lydia said. "I, Lydia, can do all this through him who gives me strength."

Pleased Lydia was learning so much from the life of Jane Ann, Grams looked at Pops and they smiled at each other.

Before leaving on their trip, Thomas L said he would take anyone who wanted to go fishing down on Honey Creek. By early afternoon, he had a wagonload of excited fishermen, cane poles, and empty air tights filled with worms.

Jane Ann, Mary Ann, Fannie, and Frances stayed behind. They wanted to take a walk to the family cemetery. Frances cut the lilac blossoms from her bushes, Mary Ann brought roses from the rose garden George planted for her, and Jane Ann gathered a bunch of daises from her garden.

The afternoon was perfect for a walk. Enjoying their time strolling along together, they picked wildflowers on the way.

Nearing the cemetery, they each had a huge bouquet of flowers. Jane Ann, whose heartache was still like an open wound, walked to Robert's grave first. The others stood behind her, giving her time to grieve. She took a deep breath and laid the beautiful flowers on his grave.

Catts - Crawford Cemetery
Established 1854

Frances placed some of her flowers on Robert's grave. Fannie and Mary Ann added more.

Mary Ann placed her flowers on George's grave. She took a few moments to let sweet memories of George's smile go through her mind.

Frances laid lilacs on her son, George's, grave and perhaps thought about her husband, John Catts.

Fannie laid down flowers in memory of her father.

Jane Ann added more flowers for her brother, George.

Then Mary Ann stepped over to little Clarence's grave. Remembering how he touched so many hearts, she placed her flowers and said, "I did have a little lamb."

Walking to the biggest oak tree, Frances put down the rest of her wildflowers and said, "These are for Charles, John Neal, and for John Catts."

Mary Ann laid the last of her flowers by the oak tree in memory of her son, John Campbell.

Jane Ann positioned her remaining flowers in memory of all soldiers.

Fannie started to cry when she laid her flowers down. Her flowers were in memory of her true love who never returned after the battle of Wilson Creek.

When they starting to leave, they glanced back at how beautiful the little cemetery looked. As Fannie closed the rusty gate, she said, "We will love them forever."

Walking back to the farmhouse, they shared their best memories and laughed the entire way home.

Late afternoon after everyone was tired, Thomas L returned to the farmhouse with a wagon full of happy people and a washtub filled with catfish. When he passed the cemetery, he pointed out to his family the beautiful flowers on the graves.

Later, after everyone had gone home, Thomas L offered to take his mother for a ride in the wagon. He didn't tell her where they were going. While riding along talking, he saw some vining wild roses. He stopped and picked a bouquet for her.

Enjoying her time with her son, Frances hadn't noticed where they were going until they rounded a corner to turn the wagon down a road not often traveled. Surprised yet pleased, she recognized they were nearing the Neely Cemetery.

Helping his mother down from the wagon, Thomas L walked with her to visit Thomas Crawford's grave. Together, they laid the bouquet of roses on his grave. Thomas L then took an apple from his pocket and laid it on his Papa's grave.

Thomas Crawford was the only father Thomas L had ever known. On their way home, time passed quickly while he and Frances shared their good memories of the husband and father they loved.

The day of remembrance was good for everyone's hearts.

In late July, after Frances, Thomas L, and Fannie returned from the Centennial, they spent many days telling their family about their memorable trip. They explained the newest and most exciting inventions called the telephone and the portable bathtub. They described how their taste-buds were tantalized as they sipped Hires Root Beer, which was like a soda-pop, tasted the banana fruit, and crunched on popped corn.

While waiting in line for popped corn, Thomas L struck up a conversation with a gentleman who said he was born in Missouri and had been a riverboat captain on the Mississippi River. His name was Samuel Clements or as most called him, Mark Twain. He told Thomas L he recently published a book about life in Missouri called, "The Adventures of Tom Sawyer."

Neither Thomas L nor Fannie knew Frances had taken the piece of the Star-Spangled Banner Flag with her to the Centennial. Hearing the flag would be on display for the celebration, she wanted to see where her piece would match on the original flag.

Respectfully, Frances approached the huge flag that once had been thirty feet by forty-two feet. Eight feet had been cut away piece by piece by Fort McHenry's Commander's wife to give to soldiers who served under the flag. Frances laid her piece as close to the flag as possible. Her piece was the right bottom corner of the flag, which was where she helped the flag maker, Mrs. Pickersgill, sew on the flag in the year 1813.

After returning home, she went to place the piece of the flag back into the rectangular wooden box. She noticed some of the fragile threads were starting to fray. Frances gathered every red and white thread and carefully laid them in the bottom of the box.

The trip had been a success for each of those who went.

The family was honored once again in 1976 when the Centennial Memorial Bracket was exhibited at America's Bicentennial Celebration.

April 1880

I couldn't help but notice while we were singing in church on Sunday, Thomas L was having trouble breathing. With each line of, "When We All Get to Heaven," he took a deep breath. Later at our family dinner, he seemed unusually tired. Never would I have imagined he was so sick. A few days later I took his favorite chicken soup with Angel Biscuits and Angel Pie topped with Chocolate Gravy to him.

When I arrive at the farm, he was in bed. Mama had been sitting with him all morning. She was thankful I brought something he might eat. Suggesting she go to her room to rest for a while, I offered to sit with Thomas L. I sat down beside him and lay cool cloths on his head in an attempt to lower his fever.

Perhaps it was the fever that made him talk so much. All afternoon he talked about our father and how he wished he would have known him. He told me he used to cry himself to sleep at night after our brother died. Reaching up to touch my face, he said, "I wish I could remember their faces."

Never having shown anyone my diary or the drawings I did of Papa and John Neal, I hesitated to show them to him. He again told me he wished he could remember their faces. I took my diary from my apron pocket and turned to the back pages. I told him they were drawings from the eyes of a young inexperienced artist and were not very good. When I showed him their faces, he seemed to be at peace.

We began to laugh about how our family adjusted to the Crawford family when Mama married Papa. And the many rotten apples we threw while learning to love each other.

We talked about our travels west and when Papa died. And we laughed for a long time while we talked about the red Catts/Crawford Christmas sleigh.

He told me about the woman he fell in love with on the wagon train and about her death. He was sad he never had his own family. I reminded him our Indian friend, Protector, named his first son Thomas. He smiled.

I told him we never would have survived during the war if he had not stayed home to take care of all of us. His courage and wisdom helped keep us safe, especially when the bushwhackers burned the farm. He seemed to be at peace as I reminded him of how many times he had been there for us. I reminded him of how many Christmas's Eves he played his fiddle for our family to dance and sing, and he laughed.

He wanted me to find the silver compass that belonged to our grandfather Neal for him from the dresser drawer. We talked about how proud he was the day he let Charles borrow it to guide him to California. A tear filled his eye when he said, "He kept his promise to give it back."

I knew he never got over Charles death. And George died so soon after Charles.

We spent hours walking down memory lane. So many wonderful memories and yet many which still made us sad.

He wanted to rest. I got Mama a chair so she too could sit with him. From her heart she thanked him for the loving care he had given her after Papa died. And thanked him for building the house, the barn, and the famous one of a kind in Lawrence County, his and her outhouses.

Thomas L smiled and squeezed her hand.

Unable to control her tears, she thanked him for the gift of the cross in the woods. It had become a place to lay down heartaches and burdens in prayer. Thomas L raised his hand and wiped away her tears.

Mama and I sat with Thomas L during the night. He did not wake the next morning.

God's servant, Thomas Love Catts, closed his eyes on April 23, 1880, and woke up in heaven. At age sixty-three, he was buried next to his beloved brother, George Catts, at the family cemetery. Most all of the town's people came to honor him as a man of faith, a good neighbor, and a friend to all. Pastor Sadie Crank officiated the service.

Mrs. Palen from church sang the song, "When We All Get to Heaven."

"A man's heart deviseth his way: but the Lord directeth his steps." (Proverbs 16:9).

God determined the steps of Thomas L which would lead him home.

After the funeral, Jane Ann folded her black gloves and placed them in the family trunk. Thomas L's was the last funeral she ever attended.

Fall 1885

My brothers have all passed away, and my children are

all grown. I have decided to move to the farm to help Mama in her last years. Even though Fannie lives with her, teaching school and church activities keep her busy. Helen Frances and her family will move into our house in town because it is close to where her husband works at the bank.

Perhaps I am getting old. I want to be sure I have my life in order and organize the treasures I want to pass on to my family. They are the things which will tell the story of my life.

I enjoy crocheting cross bookmarkers for friends and family. For those who don't know the love of God, I use the cross bookmark to explain the plan of salvation. I share John 3:16 when I give them the cross.

I spend my evenings sitting by the cozy, warm fire reading. I am thankful I did not give up my desire to learn to read when I was a child. The challenges at that time were great, but the rewards of reading, has lasted my entire lifetime. I have traveled the world through books, learned things I never thought possible, and used reading as my restful place to forget my problems, at least for a while. With reading, my imagination opened my mind to create new and exciting things. God has blessed me abundantly.

Concerned for her future, Frances encouraged Fannie to build a home of her own on the farm. Fannie drew a floorplan she would like to build. The house would be bigger than she'd need, but if necessary, she could rent the upstairs rooms.

Jane Ann enjoyed walking the fields with Fannie, often scattering wildflower seeds along the road and planting purple iris beside each tree. She would bring new life to the Catts/Crawford farm.

They have time to talk while walking. Fannie talked about going to school at the Woman's Academy in Wellsburg. She laughed when Jane Ann reminded her it was called the Girl's Academy when she attended.

Fannie shared her heartache of not knowing her brother, little Clarence, or getting more time with her father before he passed away. Jane Ann assured her without her education, a good future would have been difficult.

Jane Ann talked about the difficulties she had while learning to read and how the letters and numbers moved. She was shocked when Fannie told her the condition was called dyslexia, known as word-blindness, meaning difficulty with words.

Not knowing how to deal with it nor wanting to talk about it, Jane Ann always thought something bad was wrong with her. Her brothers didn't have the problems she had in learning to read. She was glad to know other people faced her same situations.

Fannie explained how more research was being done to help the many children who were dyslexic. Some doctors thought dyslexic children were more gifted. They excelled in other ways and were extremely intelligent. She especially wanted Jane Ann to know the famous composer, Mozart, and the painter, Leonardo da Vinci, were found to be dyslexic. Fanny told her most dyslexic people have artistic abilities and could see what other people couldn't. She said perhaps Jane Ann was an artist waiting to be discovered.

In a funny English voice, Fannie said, "You, my dear Aunt Jane Ann, are most intelligent." Then in a serious voice, she said, "And you are the kindest, most compassionate person I have ever known."

"See Lydia, we are in with some pretty special people," Grams said with a smile. "Jane Ann was one of them. By reading her diary, we have had the privilege of personally knowing her. And her life has encouraged both of us."

Lydia nodded, excited to get home and explore more about how to overcome her problems with reading.

September 6, 1888

The doctor visited with me today and thinks I have a bad case of pneumonia. That is what took my Robert and Thomas L's life. Feeling weak, I knew my soul was becoming stronger in the longing to be with those I love. I had cried so many tears as I wondered what I would do without Robert. I soon will not have that worry. I will be with him once again.

I don't know what heaven will be like. But I am certain God would not have given me the longing to see him, Robert, and others if he had not prepared a place for me. My heart is filled with love for those I will leave behind:

my children, Mama, family, and friends. I am at peace because they are secure in their faith.

Before starting to write in my diary, I turned to the back pages to see pencil drawings I did as a child—drawings of Papa Catts and John Neal. I wanted to draw their faces so I would never forget them. They stare at me from the faded pages of my diary, and I wonder what they will look like in heaven. Thomas L is the only person I ever showed my drawings to.

I flip back to the drawings of Papa, little Clarence, George, and last, Thomas L. I never would have imagined how precious the drawings would be to me.

I did not do a drawing of Robert. His handsome face is forever etched in my mind and on my heart.

I know my time will soon end, so I feel I must finish putting my life in order.

While Mama is cooking supper and thinks I am sleeping, I will neatly tuck away my treasures for someone to find. Since I am the last with the Catts/Crawford name, Mama gave me the family treasures to keep. I will use my black velvet bag to keep them together.

I was also entrusted with the wooden box Uncle John Neal made which has held the piece of the flag for many years. Sadly, all that is left are unwoven red and white threads which are in the bottom of the box.

The last cross bookmark I crocheted, I will not give away. I will instead leave it in the family Bible.

I picked up the beautiful blue broach Mama gave me for my sixtieth birthday. Since it belonged to her mother, it was always dear to her heart. I will wrap it in the handkerchief which belonged to her friend, Francis Scott

Key. I shall add the Crawford silver pocket watch which belonged to Papa's father and was given to Charles when he turned twenty-one.

Next, I will carefully include the silver writing pen Uncle John Neal gave to John Neal. It has been used by almost everyone in the family at one time or another. Even Mama used it when she signed the homestead papers on the farm.

I picked up the silver compass to lay it inside the bag. It guided the Neal family to America and the Catts/ Crawford family across our great country.

Lifting the silver baby spoon that has been passed among the family and on to me to put in the bag, I smiled. I wonder who will be given the spoon in the future.

I picked up the silver thimble—the one Mama gave me when I was learning to sew. As her mother and most likely, her grandmother did, I continued. I used it to sew beautiful hats. This sustained our family in the most difficult times. Adding the thimble last, I pulled the draw strings of the black velvet bag and laid it in the wooden box with the red and white threads.

I counted seven letters I wanted someone to read in the future and laid them in the box. They will explain more of my life.

Unable to see well, I searched in my sewing basket for a needle and thread. With it, I sewed a tiny key to the back of the last crocheted cross I made. I laid it down on the bed.

I struggled to pick up the family Bible from my bedside table. Feeling weak, I sat down on the bed. Holding God's Word to my heart, I raised my hand toward heaven and said, "Thank you, Lord" and opened the Bible to the Catts/Crawford family records.

Reading the names of the people I loved, I stared down at the pages until I read the name "Robert W. Crawford." I couldn't control the tears as they fell onto the page. Under his name I wrote my name and the date I was born. To the side of my name I wrote, "The key is in God's Word." I laid the Bible back on the bedside table.

When I finish writing in my diary, I will lock it with the key which is sewn to the cross bookmark. I will place it in the wooden box with my other treasures.

I will mark my favorite Scripture verse, Matthew 6:21, in the family Bible with the Cross bookmark.

With the key Mama gave me, I will lock the wooden box and lay the key on top. She will find it sitting on the dresser—hers to decide what to do with what is in the box. The family treasures are hers once again.

Very tired, I walked to the west window of my room to look at the family cemetery one last time. I don't think there is anything more beautiful than the evening sun slowly slipping away beyond the big oak trees around the cemetery.

As I ponder the many memories I have stored up in my heart, the last words I have are for my family I love so very much.

"The best, most wonderful gifts are not something you give away. They are the precious moments when God allows time to stop long enough for you to remember them. Every moment changed my life and brought me closer to heaven."

Jane Ann Catts/Crawford

September 6, 1888

Jane Ann spent her entire life as a compassionate and loving caregiver for her family. She loved to sew, using the thimble which once belonged to her grandmother to make clothes, quilts, and hats for others. Realizing the great need during the war, she established ladies sewing circles and distribution of food to the needy. She never saw the color of anyone's skin when they were in need. Nor did she care which side they chose to support during the war. She only wanted to help bandage their wounds and prayerfully send them home to family. Jane Ann did without to give to others.

Frances, her mother, found a note on top of the wooden box from Jane Ann. She asked to be buried wearing the gold, heart-shaped necklace with a cross in the center. She requested a heart and cross to be carved on the top of her casket along with the Scripture Matthew 6:21.

With her beautiful blue eyes looking upward toward heaven, Jane Ann Catts/Crawford, age seventy-five, peacefully passed away at the family farm south of Mount Vernon.

Her obituary said, "Those who knew her best did not dream the death angel was hovering so near. She was a faithful and devoted member of the Christian Church and well did she prove her faith; if she could possibly get there, her seat in church or prayer meetings was never vacant, Jane Ann was respected by all who knew her and loved most by those who knew her best. She was a faithful daughter to an aged mother, a loving and devoted wife and mother to her children. May her blessed example and loving precepts be with them and may they so live that their parting will be but for a season, and they will meet in the sweet bye and bye."

Jane Ann Catts/Crawford was buried beside her beloved husband, Robert.

"For where your treasure is, Jane Ann, there your heart will be also" (Matthew 6:21).

Jane Ann left a cookbook she wrote for Fannie on the kitchen table under a bowl of apples. The cover was sewn with red-gingham fabric. On the front was embroidered in red, "Thou art my portion, O Lord" (Psalm 119:57).

On the first page of the cookbook, Jane Ann wrote, "I am homeward bound, and I will never pass this way again. My love and prayers remain with you. Aunt Jane Ann Catts/Crawford."

MS. PRISCILLA'S ANGEL BISCUITS WITH COKEY'S CHOCOLATE GRAVY

5 Cups flour
¾ Cup shortening
3 Tsp baking powder
2 Cups buttermilk
1 tsp salt
2 packages active dry yeast
1 tsp soda
½ warm water
3 Tbs sugar
2 sticks butter, cold, cut into small squares, plus ½ stick melted butter
Directions:
In a small bowl, dissolve yeast in warm water. It will look like paste.

Combine dry ingredients in large bowl. Mix with a whisk.

Cut butter into chunks, add to dry ingredients and use fingers to break into tiny pieces.

Stir the yeast paste into the buttermilk and add to biscuit dough. Mix with a wooden spoon and then knead dough with hands to be sure it is mixed well.

Sprinkle flour on a large sheet of wax paper. Gently pat and fold the dough into a rectangle 1 inch thick several times.

Brush melted butter in a large cast iron skillet and set aside.

Pat dough again 1 inch thick. Use a biscuit cutter or glass to cut dough into circles.

Place biscuits in skillet so they touch slightly. Cover with plastic and let rise in skillet for 1 hour.

15 minutes before hour is up, preheat oven to 400 degrees F.

Brush raised biscuits with melted butter and bake for 15 minutes or until golden brown.

Cool before removing from skillet. Serve with honey butter or homemade jelly.

If you have left over cold biscuits, try serving with Chocolate Gravy.

COKEY'S CHOCOLATE GRAVY

2 Tbs cocoa
2 Tbs flour
4 Tbs sugar
1 Cup milk
1 tsp vanilla

Combine ingredients in a skillet. Mix well with a wire whisk. Cook on medium heat.

When gravy thickens, pour on top of cold biscuits.

EPILOGUE

Lydia took a deep breath and said, "Grams, I hope God gives me a heart like Jane Ann. Her life has encouraged me to be determined to find a way to deal with being dyslexic and to help others who struggle as I do. We'll be the ones who'll solve the problem for future generations."

Grams, Lydia, and Pops sat in silence.

Finally, Lydia said, "I think I know what the three keys to life Jane Ann's mother talked about might be. They are faith, hope, and love. She lived her faith and never allowed it to be silent. Her hope was forever, and God's love never failed her."

The next morning, the three of them finished sanding and oiling the walnut bedroom set from the barn. They looked at it with different eyes and with more appreciation. They realized they had found a friend named Jane Ann. The life lessons from her diary would stay with Lydia for the rest of her life.

What once embarrassed Lydia became a challenge she would meet with confidence. She now saw being dyslexic as a gift to see what others could never imagine.

After she returned home with the beautiful walnut bedroom set for her room, Lydia found two surprises from Pops and Grams in one of the drawers. One was Jane Ann's diary which she treasured. The other was an envelope with Priscilla Rose's name on it. Inside was a list of the items they found in the bench. Pops wrote at the bottom, "Maybe this is your story."

Grams bought Lydia a diary for her birthday. On the inside she wrote, "Just a moment changes life forever. With love and prayers, Grams and Pops"

ABOUT THE AUTHOR

Billie Fulton, a writer from Springfield, Missouri, believes our first response to circumstances is always our heart response. Who we are in our heart comes out when faced with split-second decisions. After raising her family and spending years working in Women's Ministry in her church, she is following her dream to write about the hearts of real people in real times. She finds the challenges they faced, or that we face, are no different than people in the Bible. But as with them, our heart response to failure or success is how we learn. She is teaming with the love of her life, John Fulton, an accomplished artist, to visually compliment her writing. She treasures their time together and always finds time to dance in the bubbles with her grandchildren.

ABOUT THE ILLUSTRATOR

John Fulton is an accomplished watercolor artist from Springfield, Missouri. His commissioned collage paintings hang in both corporate and private collections nationally and internationally.

His unique style of visually displaying the heritage and attributes of a corporation or organization has allowed his work to be used on book covers, brochures and limited edition prints. He most enjoys using his God given talent to illustrate books with his wife Billie.

Made in the USA
Monee, IL
23 March 2021

63535694R00140